Alaska Williwaw #1

Murphy
and the Mystery of the Black Skull

Bradford D. Smith

Fathom Publishing Company

Anchorage, Alaska

Copyright © 2024 Bradford D. Smith

All rights reserved. No part of this book or any subsequent editions may be reproduced, transmitted, broadcast or stored in an informational retrieval system in any form or by any means, graphics, electronic or mechanical, including photocopying or photographing, without the written permission from the publisher, except for the inclusion of brief quotations in an acknowledged review. Requests for permission or further information should be addressed to the author.

ISBN 978-1-954896-96-3 Paperback
ISBN 978-1-954896-97-0 ebook

Cover Design Argeo Jobim

Printed in United States of America

This is a work of fiction. Names, characters, businesses, places, events, locales, and incidents are either the products of the author's imagination or used in a fictitious manner. Any resemblance to actual persons, living or dead, or actual events is purely coincidental.

Some locales or buildings, such as Juneau and Douglas, Alaska, and Gastineau Channel exist. They are only the setting for the fictional events portrayed in the Williwaw Mystery Series.

Fathom Publishing Company
PO Box 200448 | Anchorage, Alaska 99520
FathomPublishing.com

To Delilah and Daisy

Contents

Chapter 1: Pirates

Murphy tossed and turned in his bed as a violent storm raged. Sometimes storms scared him. He was dreaming about pirates, an octopus with shoes, blue kangaroos, and a gigantic yellow jellyfish. The jellyfish was stuck to his face, he couldn't breathe. It was slimy and sticky and smelled like dog food.

Dog food?

He woke with a start, drawing in a deep breath and opening his eyes just in time to see an enormous, pink snake lunge at his face. He ducked under the covers to escape the attack.

"Hogan! What are you doing?"

Hogan was the family dog. A boxer with big white feet, huge buggy eyes, a stubby tail and short beige fur. Murphy's parents were convinced Hogan thought he was human. Maybe even Murphy's brother, who knows. Licking was one of Hogan's favorite things and he loved to lick Murphy the most.

Hogan was playful, but he could be serious when he needed to be. Murphy could tell this was one of those serious times. He stifled a yawn. Hogan clearly had something important on his mind. "What are you doing up so late?"

Hogan ran to the half-open bedroom door and looked back expectantly.

"All right, I'm coming." Murphy struggled to free himself from tangled blankets and jumbled pillows. He caught a glimpse of Hogan's rear end as he disappeared into the darkened living room. "Wait for me, Hoge!"

Murphy shuffled into the living room in his PJs. Lately he'd been thinking he was getting too old for pajamas. His friend Mikey said he slept in his underwear and only little kids wore pajamas.

"Where are you, boy? Be quiet or you'll wake up Kat," he whispered. Sounds came from the corner by the big front window. "Hogan, what are you doing over there?"

Hogan stood on his back legs, his forepaws on the windowsill. His nose pressed the glass as he stared intently through the rain-streaked pane at the water beyond. A low rumble emanated from deep within his chest. Hogan only growled when he sensed danger.

"What is it, Hoge? What's the matter, boy? What are you looking at?"

Murphy's house sat on pilings over the beach on the shore of Gastineau Channel. At high tide, waves washed underneath the floor. On clear nights, they could see the lights of downtown Juneau.

Murphy pressed his face to the window and peered into the inky blackness. Wind and rain pummeled the side of the house. Water ran in torrents down the glass. Under his feet, he felt his home swaying from side to side as it struggled to repel Mother Nature's tumultuous onslaught. It reminded him of the williwaws they sometimes experienced. The sudden violent squalls sweeping down from the mountainsides were always shocking and often dangerous.

Through the distorted pane, Murphy saw a tiny light bobbing in the channel. It wasn't very bright, but the longer he stared, the clearer it became.

That's strange. Who would be out on a night like this? That lantern is just like the ones Dad sells in his antique shop.

As his eyes became accustomed to the gloom, he noticed the lantern hung from the rigging of an old wooden ship. The lantern swung back and forth as the ancient vessel rose and fell in the waves. The sail was down and wrapped tightly around the lower yardarm. The anchor was set, and the chain was taut, holding the ship in place against the gale. A large black flag flew from the top of the mast. It flapped maniacally in the wind.

Out of the corner of his eye, he caught the glint of another light. He rushed to the side window with Hogan close behind. On the flat sandy beach, not far from the house, four men stood beside a small skiff. The little boat was tied to an old rotten piling a couple yards up a small stream. The men stood with their backs to the wind, so Murphy couldn't see their faces. They wore what appeared to be dark green rain gear and rubber boots. Two of the men carried shovels, one held another antique lantern, and the fourth man, who was much larger than the others, clutched a strange object. It had a round disk on one end and a small square box on the other.

Murphy observed as the men loaded the shovels and other items into the skiff. Three men scrambled aboard while the last, a very tall man, untied the bow line from the piling and shoved the skiff down the creek and off the beach. At the last minute, he hopped aboard. The waves and rain buffeted the men and their boat. It was all two men with the oars could do to turn the skiff around and keep it from washing back onto the beach.

Murphy watched as the men strained mightily on the oars and struggled to keep the skiff pointed toward their ship.

Movement on the deck of the larger vessel caught his attention. A lone dark figure leaned over the rail. As the skiff approached amidship, the tall man tossed up the bow line. The lone figure caught it and snubbed it around the ship's rail. This man was stocky and squat, where the men in the skiff were much taller.

He watched as the skiff bumped and ground against the hull of the ship while the men scrambled aboard. Once they were safely on the deck, the lone man untied the skiff's line, grasped it firmly in both hands and shuffled aft, allowing the skiff to drift astern of the larger vessel. He played out line until the skiff rode lightly on the waves directly behind the ship. The man passed the line through a scupper and made it fast around an aft deck cleat. Finished with his task, he joined his fellows.

There are pirates outside, right in front of our house!

Murphy gawked as the men bustled around the deck, preparing to make way. The men kept their hoods up, so no matter how hard he tried, he could not see their faces.

He looked down at Hogan. "Did you see what I saw?"

Hogan wiggled his rear and licked Murphy's hand.

"Hey, what are you guys doing up?"

Murphy jumped and let out a startled yelp. Hogan spun around and emitted a low woof.

Murphy turned to see his cousin Katrina standing behind him. She was rubbing her eyes and brushing errant wisps of fuchsia-colored hair from her face.

"What's going on? It's the middle of the night."

Murphy and Katrina were not really cousins, but their fathers were lifelong friends and, as far as anyone was concerned, they were family.

"There are pirates out there and a pirate ship! I'm going to go get my dad. Look for yourself. I'll be right back." Murphy rushed past her, bounded across the living room, and launched himself over the sofa. He landed lightly and ran down the hallway. Hogan skirted the couch, knowing he wasn't allowed on it, and was on Murphy's heels.

They bumped and shoved against each other and burst into his parents' bedroom in a blur of arms, legs, hands, and paws.

"Mom! Dad! Wake up! There are pirates outside!"

His mom, Sonia, raised her head from her pillow, groaned and rubbed sleep from her eyes. She absently brushed long strands of jet-black hair from her face. "Shhhhh, keep it down. If you wake up Katrina, I will personally make you walk the plank."

"Woops, too late. Sorry, Mom; she's already up. I think Hogan woke her up, too."

His dad's gruff voice, thick with sleep, radiated from deep within the covers.

"Not pirates again, Murph?"

Murphy shook his head. "No, they're outside, come and see. Wake up, Dad! Come and see the pirates! They're real, it's not a dream this time. They have a ship and everything. Just ask Hogan, he saw them too, right, boy?"

Hogan shook his rump and wagged his tongue, drooling in his excitement. He put his feet on the bed and licked Murphy's dad's ear, the only part he could reach.

"Hogan, get down," his dad thundered, sitting upright and wiping Hogan's slobber from the side of his face.

Murphy often thought his dad looked like a pirate, especially when he was tired or cranky. He had a gold earring like pirates do and he routinely said "Arrrrg" when he was frustrated. Sometimes he wore a bandana on his head, and he had one eye that wandered. With his jet-black hair and day-old stubble, he could easily pass for a character out of any pirate movie. His name was John, like Long John Silver from *Treasure Island*, one of Murphy's favorite books. But even if his dad were a real pirate, Murphy knew he wouldn't be mean and scary like Captain Hook.

"Come on," Murphy pleaded, "let's go. It's anchored right in front of the house. The pirates have shovels, a pirate flag, and everything! Please, Dad, you have to come and see. Hurry, they're leaving."

Sonia nudged John in the ribs and muttered, "It's your turn, dear. I put him back to bed last time." She yanked the covers over her head. "Good night, Murph. I love you. Dad is going to tuck you back in."

As John swung his feet over the side of the bed, her muffled voice emanated from under the covers. "Tuck Katrina back in, too, hon. The poor thing was rudely woken up by a couple yahoos in the middle of the night. You owe her an apology in the morning, Murphy."

"Yes, I will," John muttered while rubbing an eye with one hand and blindly searching for a slipper with the other.

"It was Hogan, not me." Murphy complained.

Hogan looked up at Murphy with big sad eyes.

John climbed out of bed. "Come on, Murph. Let's go see your pirates." Yawning, he put on his robe and slipped his feet into the Sponge Bob slippers that Murphy had given him for his birthday. He took Murphy by the hand and the three of them left the bedroom and headed to the front of the house.

Murphy pulled at his dad impatiently. As they entered the living room, Katrina sat up from her makeshift bed on the love seat in the corner.

"What is it now? Is there a space ship outside? Have the aliens arrived to take Murphy and Hogan home?" Katrina giggled softly.

Murphy hurried to the big picture window. The ship was gone. "Very funny, Kat. Where did they go?"

Murphy ran to the side window and strained to find the small skiff or the four men, but of course, they weren't there.

"They're gone," he said disappointedly.

"There was a pirate ship, Dad, and four men, and a small skiff and they had shovels and some other weird thing."

Murphy leaned closer to the glass, trying to see where the men pushed off in their skiff. "They were right there." He pointed into the darkness. "Honest they were. Their skiff was tied up to that old piling beside the small stream." Tears of frustration welled in his hazel eyes as he continued to point in vain.

"Another man waited on the ship for them. Maybe he was the captain." Murphy sighed. "Kat saw them too, right, Kat?"

"Well, I saw a ship and some men but it looked more like a sus old fishing boat to me, not a pirate ship."

"Come on, it had a mast and a sail. What fishing boats have sails?" Murphy protested.

"I don't know, it's black out there and the rain makes it hard to see. I guess it could have been pirates, because that's like totally normal." She smiled at Murphy. "I'm going back to sleep."

Katrina turned, walked to the love seat and crawled under a fluffy down comforter. She turned away from them, and faced the wall.

John rested his hand on his son's shoulder. "Come on, let's get you back to bed."

"But what about the flag, Dad?"

"What flag?"

"The big black flag. The ship, it had a big black flag flying from its mast. I couldn't see very well in the dark but I'll bet it had a skull and cross bones on it. Besides fishing boats don't fly flags and only pirates fly a black flag, right?"

"Well, I guess that's true, only pirates fly the black flag. We can talk more about it in the morning." He steered his son toward his bedroom.

Murphy stopped at his door. "I did see pirates, Dad, and so did Hogan and so did Kat even if she doesn't understand what she saw."

"I heard that," a sleepy voice wafted in from the darkened living room.

Murphy lowered his voice. "Hogan saw them first and woke me up. Just ask him. Right, Hoge?" He glanced around for Hogan, but the dog was nowhere to be found.

Great, now he's not even going to help me.

Entering his room, Murphy saw Hogan's rear end sticking out from behind a beanbag chair.

Thanks a lot, Hogan. You're a big help. You got me into this, then you run and hide when I really need you.

His dad tucked him in and kissed his cheek. "Goodnight, Murph, I'll see you in the morning." He turned to leave.

"It had a name you know."

"What did?"

"The ship did. It was called the *Black Skull.*"

"That's nice. Sleep well, I'll see you in the morning. Love you."

"Love you, too, Dad. And it really was there."

"We'll talk about it tomorrow. Good night."

Murphy rolled over just in time to see Hogan wiggle his way from behind the beanbag chair and curl up on the floor next to the bed.

"Now you're here. Where were you when I needed you?"

Hogan hid his nose under one paw and looked up at Murphy as if to say sorry. Murphy reached down and scratched his ears. "Good night, Hoge. At least you believe me."

Hogan wiggled his butt and licked Murphy's hand. While he pondered the recent events, Murphy yawned and lay back on his pillow. He felt a mounting compulsion to solve the mystery of the pirates.

What happened and what did I really see? How can I figure it out?

Chapter 2: School Days

Next morning on the school bus, Murphy could hardly contain his excitement. He couldn't wait to tell his friends about the pirate ship. He wanted to talk with Kat about it, but when you are twelve, you don't sit by a girl on the bus, and you certainly don't talk to her in front of her friends, or yours.

As soon as the bus door opened, Murphy was off and running across the school yard toward the monkey bars. He and his friends had made the monkey bars their official hang out and rallying place. He was happy to see his friend Mikey already perched atop the rectangular maze of bars.

Murphy loved climbing. He enjoyed using his considerable strength and agility, and both served him well in climbing and his favorite sport, wrestling. Murphy ascended nimbly and sat by his friend. "Guess what I saw last night."

"Did your dad finally let you watch *Horror Hollow III*? I can't believe he won't let you see it, everyone else has."

"No, it's way better than a scary movie. I saw a pirate ship."

"You saw a pirate ship? Where?"

"In the channel right in front of our house. Hogan woke me up and Kat, er, Katrina, saw it, too."

A light gust of wind ruffled Murphy's short tawny hair. It chilled him slightly and he zipped up his jacket.

"Did she stay at your place again? Your parents may as well adopt her; she's there all the time. It must be terribad having her around."

"She's okay, I mean for a girl. You know my Uncle Jerry, her dad, he's a crabber, he's gone a lot, so she stays with us. Anyway, there was a pirate ship anchored in front of our house last night in the middle of the storm and there were men and a skiff and a black flag and everything."

"That's fire. Did they have muskets, did they have eye patches or did one have a hook or a wooden leg? Was Peter there or Wendy? I know, I bet Tinkerbell sprinkled pixie dust on you?" Mikey grinned from ear to ear, freckles covering his plump cheeks, their rusty color matching his hair. "That's a good one, Murphy. Did you stay up all night thinking it up? Nothing sketchy here, only pirates and fairies." Mikey laughed at his own joke.

"Real funny, Mikey. There weren't any fairies and I know what I saw and it was a pirate ship with real pirates."

Throughout the day, he tried to tell his friends about what he'd seen, but they all reacted much like Mikey had. If not outright taunts and general buffoonery, Murphy's story was met with disinterest and disdain. Murphy hated it. Especially from his close friends. It frustrated him, but it also sparked his dogged determination. His dad called it his inner pit bull.

After school, he sat at the breakfast bar with his mom eating a peanut butter and jelly sandwich and drinking a glass of milk. He told her about his day and his frustrations with his friends.

Sonia casually flipped through the newspaper as she listened. Her glasses slowly slid down her nose and she pushed them up with a slender finger.

"You know Brandon and Caleb?" Murphy asked.

"Yes, I do, they're in your Junior Geologist Club, aren't they?" She folded the paper.

"Yeah, they are. They tried to blindfold me and make me walk the plank. Well, the teeter totter anyway. And Josh W. screamed 'arrrrgggg' in my ear all day. Brandon kept asking me where my eye patch was. Everyone was hitting my legs to see if one was wooden. Plus, they wanted to know if I had a hook. And Mikey, he's supposed to be my best friend, he was the worst. He called me Captain Murphy Beard all day."

Sonia smirked and turned away.

"It's not funny, Mom."

She turned back to Murphy. "I know, honey, it's never easy to be picked on but I think your buddies are just having a bit of fun with you. They will probably have forgotten by tomorrow. Captain Murphy Beard is a little funny, you have to admit." A smile tugged at the corners of her mouth and her ebony pupils sparkled mischievously.

Murphy smiled too. "Okay, that is a little funny. Kat saw them too even if she doesn't know what she saw and won't admit it. It was obviously a pirate ship and a gang of pirates." Murphy heard the neighbor's dog barking next door.

"I'm sorry you had such a bad day, Murph. Next time you see pirates, don't tell anyone except me and your dad. We believe you."

"Do you, Mom? Do you believe I saw a real live pirate ship right outside our house?"

"You believe you saw a real live pirate ship last night right outside our house. That's good enough for me."

But not good enough for anyone else. Now what do I do?

Chapter 3: Mr. Fisher

Murphy was determined to solve the mystery of the pirate ship. The name he remembered from the bow stuck in his head and he repeated it over and over: *Black Skull, Black Skull.* Somehow it seemed familiar. A distant memory tickled the far reaches of his brain. The feeling he'd heard that name mentioned or had seen it written down somewhere would not leave him.

But how? Where?

Murphy's dad collected antiques, books, and documents from the Klondike Gold Rush. He'd read many of those books to Murphy over the years as they shared an enthusiasm for northern history.

John was a local history expert and owned his own antique shop downtown. As a student, he had worked at Juneau Books and was mentored by long-time Juneau historian and Juneau Books owner, Ned Fisher.

Murphy wouldn't be able to pick his dad's brain for a couple days until he got back from his conference in Anchorage. So he decided to call Mr. Fisher.

If anybody would know about a pirate ship, or any ship named *Black Skull,* it would be Mr. Fisher. He was retired now but remained active in the Historical Society and the Friends of

Wooden Boats Association. And he was the long-time president of the Juneau Yacht Club.

In his youth, Mr. Fisher had been an expert sailor and navigator. For many years, he had worked with cartographers mapping Gastineau Channel's rugged coastline, successfully navigating through some of the world's most dangerous waters in all types of weather.

Murphy borrowed his mom's cell phone. "Mom, if I had my own phone—"

"I know, Murphy," she interrupted. "I've heard it all before. Good things come to the patient."

I'll be a patient in an old folks' home before I get my own phone.

He would rather have texted like almost everyone he knew would have, but Mr. Fisher didn't own a cell phone.

"Hey, Mr. Fisher, it's Murphy." He raised his voice because Mr. Fisher was hard of hearing.

Fisher replied with his usual boisterous greeting. "I would know that voice anywhere. Hello, son, how are you today?" He always called him son, but he called pretty much everyone son. "When are you going to bring your parents by for a proper visit?" His voice boomed from deep within his expansive belly and rumbled through the phone. "I haven't seen you guys in weeks."

"My dad's in Anchorage, but I'll ask my mom when I get off the phone."

"Oh, yes, I should have remembered. The annual Vintage Book Fair is being held at the Sullivan Arena this weekend. You know I took your dad to his first one many years ago."

"I remember him telling me." Murphy replied.

"Hey, make sure you let your mom know I caught a perfect eating-size halibut yesterday and my cherry tomatoes are ripe. When your dad gets back, we'll grill up some fish and I'll make a green house salad. How's that sound?"

"Sound good to me and I've got to show you my moonstone crystal I found on Mount Roberts."

"What's that, son?"

Murphy repeated himself louder.

"Hey, that's exciting Murph, I can't wait to see it."

Mr. Fisher lived alone now. His wife of thirty-six years, Edna, passed away five years earlier. She was the love of his life and he hadn't been the same since her death. Although he was still quick to laugh and always ready with a joke, Murphy's mom said that special twinkle in his eyes had faded away.

"I'll be looking forward to a nice visit. This old house could use a youngster's laughter now and again." Mr. Fisher's voice boomed from the phone. "I'm not complaining Murphy, but it is not like you to call, is everything all right?"

When Murphy didn't answer immediately, Mr. Fisher said, "Usually, it's your dad calling me with a question that only someone of my learned esteem might know the answer to." He barked a short laugh at his own joke. "I'm sure you know how I love to show off my vast knowledge of everything old and moldy."

Murphy heard barking from outside the house. It sounded like Fluffy, Mrs. Ivanov's English Bulldog. Hogan barked once in the kitchen and Murphy heard his mom's muffled admonishment.

"I actually have a question for you, Mr. Fisher, but you have to promise not to laugh."

"I promise. No laughing. Now out with it."

Murphy told the whole story, starting from Hogan waking him up. He explained the men, the strange object, the black flag, Katrina thinking it was only a fishing boat and even how his friends had treated him at school. He left out the name of the ship until the very end.

"For some reason, I can't get the name, *Black Skull,* out of my head. Is there some way my dad read something about it to me in one of his old books? Did you ever hear about a ship called the *Black Skull,* Mr. Fisher?" Murphy heard Fluffy bark again.

There was a long silence on the other end of the line before Mr. Fisher began to speak. "As far as I know, there were never any pirates this far north, or in this part of the world for that matter, and certainly no pirate ships.

"There was a rumor told many years ago when I was a young man. A salvage crew from Seattle was in town that summer attempting to retrieve the purported ton of Klondike gold that went down on the SS *Islander.*"

Murphy heard him clear his throat and take a sip of a drink. The ice cubes jingled in his glass. "My dad read me a book about the *Islander.* It's crazy that it hit an ice burg and wrecked right here on Douglas Island only a couple miles from our house."

"Yes, it is, and there were other spectacular wrecks on and around Douglas Island in the old days. Anyway, the salvage attempt stirred up all kinds of rumors and outright lies. Suddenly half the town had a story to tell."

Murphy heard him take another drink.

"When the salvage crew didn't find much, that's when the pirate rumors started. People actually believed pirates were a valid reason the gold was gone. Can you believe that?" Fisher barked out a short loud laugh.

Murphy held the phone away from his ear, but could hear when the laugh ended and was followed by a muffled cough and the clink of ice cubes. After a few seconds of quiet, he brought the phone back to his ear.

"As a young boy I helped my father when he and his crew hung gill nets and re-webbed crab pots. I loved listening to the men as they told sea stories, as my father called them." His voice trailed off and the silence was filled with the dog barking outside.

Murphy heard Mr. Fisher take a deep breath.

"One day, two of the crew spoke of pirates and a ship that flew the black flag. I was, of course, immediately fascinated. That night I asked my father about it, but he laughed and said they were only stories that no one should believe. I've never heard anything about a ship called the *Black Skull* though, not even rumors." Fisher's voice trailed off again. "The SS *Princess May* was said to have over six million in Klondike nuggets when she went down. Maybe she was a victim of pirates as well."

Fisher chuckled quietly. "Your dad knows all this history from reading the books in my store instead of dusting and stocking them. He thought I didn't notice. Who was I to interrupt a young man's free education? Somehow, he always got his work done. And now he's passing that knowledge down to you."

Murphy heard the jingle of the ice cubes. "He sure does know a lot about Alaska history, but he said he learned it all from you, Mr. Fisher. I'll ask him when he gets back though."

"Good idea, Murph. I truly hope you find your pirates and the mysterious *Black Skull*. Keep in mind, as you described, visibility was poor and it could be possible you saw an old derelict fishing vessel, so don't get your hopes up too high."

"But I saw a pirate ship and it was flying a black flag and it was called the *Black Skull* plain as day and you just said there was a pirate ship here a long time ago and it was flying a black flag."

"My dad said they were only stories, and that was decades ago. It's improbable it could be the same one you saw, son."

"I don't know, Mr. Fisher, but the ship I saw was a real pirate ship, the pirates are real and I'll figure out how to prove it."

"I admire your tenacity, son."

Murphy heard him take another drink and smack his lips.

"To me, son, geology sounds like a faster way to find gold than looking for pirate treasure."

"Treasure would be awesome, but right now I just want to find the pirates or their ship."

"Well, Murphy, if anyone can, I'm sure you can. Anyway, I hope I helped. Thanks for calling me and I'm excited to see your moonstone crystal. I've got a couple new transportation stamps I want to show you. Don't forget to tell your mom about the halibut, actually just ask her to call me."

"I will. Thanks, Mr. Fisher, see you soon."

Murphy hung up. He was excited and frustrated by the call. He was excited there was at least a story of pirates and a pirate ship in Alaska, but frustrated it was about an event that took place so long ago

There's no way it could be the same ship, could it?

Chapter 4: Unexplained Holes

Rain gurgled in the downspouts as Murphy returned to the kitchen and gave his mom her phone. He was quiet, thinking of what Mr. Fisher told him about the story of a pirate ship around Douglas Island so many years earlier. He finished his milk and put the glass in the dishwasher while Sonia read the newspaper.

"This is strange."

"What's strange, Mom?"

She pointed to an article on the front page and began reading aloud.

Unexplained Holes Appear

Mrs. Jones awoke this morning to discover several large holes in her yard. They were apparently dug clandestinely last night during one of the worst gales Gastineau Channel has experienced this year. And this is not the first incident. Five other times this year, people have discovered mysterious holes in their yards. The first report was down on Salmon Creek, early this spring.

Sonia looked at Murphy and pushed her glasses up her narrow nose. "Mrs. Jones lives down the beach and up the hill. That little stream beside our house runs behind her place before it cuts across the beach and comes out right here." She pointed out the window where Murphy had seen the pirates and their skiff.

"I know, Mom. Me and Caleb waded up it last summer all the way to her yard. We waded up a couple others, too."

"Who do you think would sneak into people's yards at night to dig holes? And why? And the holes all here in Douglas along the beach north of us. It all seems so strange."

"I know who, Mom."

"You do?" She peered at him over the top of the paper.

"Yep, I do. I bet it was the pirates." He grinned. "And they're probably burying treasure."

A rainbow prism danced across the wall beside the kitchen counter, catching Murphy's eye. A slight breeze moved the crystal wind chime on the deck as a stray ray of sunlight penetrated the dense cloud cover.

"Most likely someone got a new metal detector and is looking for old antiques or gold nuggets from the mines and mills that covered this area a hundred years ago," Sonia said.

"A metal detector. That's what it was, Mom. The big pirate had one. So they're looking for something and they're digging up yards to find it."

"Maybe! People do love old junk. Just ask your dad."

Murphy pretended to sound like his dad and deepened his voice. "It's rusty gold, dear."

"I know, I know, how could I forget?" She laughed. "Gold has been known to cause some strange behavior. People can get carried away searching for it."

"Gold fever, huh."

"Yes, gold fever. The town fire in 1937 destroyed the homes of over six hundred residents, so the ground around here is saturated with odd bits of junk. Every once in a while, people get excited about digging around for coins or gold nuggets, and even old bottles."

"Douglas sure has changed a lot. I can't believe it was so big. It must have been pretty cool when you grew up here, like a hundred years ago, huh, Mom?"

"Hey, smarty, I'm not that old but it was cool and even cooler when your grandma grew up here. Back then, Douglas had its own dairy, a theater, a bowling alley and a swimming pool."

"Mom, a swimming pool would be so awesome."

"Yes, it would. It was closed by the time I came along but there were a whole lot more wharfs and buildings back when I was your age. Now all that's left are those rotting pilings scattered along the shore."

"Like that one out there where the pirates tied up their skiff." He pointed out the side window. "I wish I lived here back then. Me and my friends would be at the pool all day every day."

"Back then didn't have video games, Internet, or 3D scary movies, kiddo."

"Okay, how about just having a swimming pool here now? That would work." He smiled.

"Remember when your uncle Jerry got the gold bug a couple of summers ago? He was all over the beach around here, beeping and digging and swearing and digging and beeping and swearing." She laughed. "Most people are nice enough to stay on public property."

"Uncle Jerry sure does like to swear, huh, Mom?"

"Yes, he does, but you better not repeat any of the things he says or you'll be grounded for a month."

"Don't worry about that, Mom. Did he ever find anything?"

"Uncle Jerry? Aside from a huge pile of nails, spikes, and nuts and bolts, he found a couple of damaged coins that weren't worth anything. I don't think anyone has ever found much of value, but it doesn't stop them from trying."

"Well, holes being dug at night is pretty sus, but a pirate ship is a way cooler mystery and I'm going to solve it and Mikey can bite me."

"Hey, be nice."

"Sorry, Mom, but I'll show him, I just need to figure out how." He gazed past his mom out the window where he had seen the *Black Skull* the night before.

Sonia spoke. "I guess if I was trying to solve a history mystery I might start at the museum. Mrs. Sutter should be able to help. She's pretty knowledgeable, she loves a challenge and she loves young people."

"Good idea, Mom, she does know a lot of history. Maybe she knows about the *Black Skull*."

Sonia wiped down the breakfast bar with a wet dish rag as she was talking. "She only works Saturdays now; she's semi-retired. You should ask Katrina if she wants to go, she's here all this coming week."

"Okay, cool. I'll ask her."

"Why don't you guys ride your bikes over? You never know, maybe there's something about your mystery ship in the archives."

Murphy loved going to the museum, and hanging out with Kat was kinda okay. She was a girl, but she was the only girl on the wrestling team and he thought that was pretty neat.

Chapter 5: Trip to the Museum

The rest of the week went by slowly for Murphy. Saturday morning finally arrived and he was excited. After a hasty breakfast, Murphy and Katrina grabbed their helmets and jackets and headed out the door.

"Be careful and stay on the path," his mom yelled as they slammed the door.

The sun was out and it was already warm for a Juneau summer day. There was a slight breeze rustling the leaves on the tall cottonwood trees across the street.

Murphy's bike was a cherry red BMX-style, trail rider with black rims and knobby tires. His mat-black helmet was like the kind rock climbers used. He thought it looked way cooler than the weird wedge helmets most kids wore. He decided to stuff his jacket in the small blue backpack he was seldom without. He threw it on, cinched up the chest strap, buckled his helmet and turned to see if Katrina was ready.

Katrina buckled up a neon green helmet that sported a twelve-inch safety orange mohawk. Wisps of fuchsia hair poked out beneath the rim of her helmet. Resting on her petite nose was pair of mirrored, round aviator sun glasses.

Murphy could see his reflection perfectly. His fingers quickly flew to his face where he frantically rubbed at a spot of jam on his left cheek.

Katrina's bike was a fat-tire beach cruiser. Like her helmet, it was neon green, accented with a purple seat, handlebar grips and a basket. To top it off, a shiny chrome horn was mounted on the handlebar.

For Murphy, it was all too much and the horn was the worst, but he kept his thoughts to himself. He had learned the hard way a number of times: you don't make fun of Katrina's fashion or accessory choices. On their last ride together, he had teased her about her annoying horn. For the entire ride to the park, she tooted her horn mercilessly just to get even for his criticism.

They rode by the Perseverance Theater and the Tlingit cemetery at Larson Creek. They stopped at their favorite convenience store near the bridge to get a bottle of water and watch as a fishing vessel passed beneath them under the Juneau Douglas Bridge.

Whale Project Park was a place Murphy and Katrina both loved and was a source of pride for both cities. A life-size bronze statue of a humpback whale breaching from a tranquility pond was the center piece of the park and a magnet to anyone passing by.

They sat on the edge of the pool drinking their water and marveling at the magnificent spectacle. Every so often the tranquil water began to roil and that was immediately followed by a geyser shooting skyward around the sculpture, simulating a breach. Murphy and Katrina waited until the last possible moment before running out of the splash zone as water cascaded behind them.

They spent an hour playing at Whale Project Park. Murphy was a little slow on one hasty retreat from the erupting water fountain and he ended up getting mostly drenched for his failure, much to the delight of a giggling Katrina.

It was time to go see Mrs. Sutter. Murphy figured if they walked, his shorts and t-shirt would dry out before they got to the museum, so they pushed their bikes along the walking path toward the center of town. As they meandered past the Coast Guard base, they could see the bright white hulk of the USCG Cutter *Anthony Petit* moored to the wharf. Murphy had heard on the radio that it was in town for the weekend, visiting from Ketchikan, its home port.

"I just finished a model of a cutter like that with my dad. See that gun on the bow; that's a deck mounted turret gun." He pointed at the bow of the cutter.

Katrina faked a yawn. "You make models? That's so last century."

"Hey, lots of people build models."

"If you say so."

They took a left at the Hanger on the Wharf, crossed Egan Drive and pushed their bikes up Main Street toward the Juneau Douglas City Museum on Fourth Street. Across Main from the museum sat the imposing six-story State Capital building with its four massive granite columns at the entrance.

Katrina stared at the museum as they approached. "I've always thought it looks more like someone's house than a museum."

"My dad said it was a library before."

"Really? That's cool."

Murphy stopped to gaze up the tall totem pole that stood as a dignified sentinel proudly protecting the humble house of history.

They put their bikes in the rack and hung their helmets on the handlebars, then followed the blue railing to the entry of the modest two-story burnt yellow building.

They pushed open the double glass doors and entered. Both of them knew their way around. They had visited many times on school field trips and their dads loved the place.

Katrina made a bee line to the Tlingit exhibit.

Murphy quietly called behind her. "Hey where are you going? The ship stuff is in the back by the gold mining display."

Katrina stopped and turned back. "I agreed to come with you, but I'm not looking for pirate ships, or should I say shady fishing boats."

"It wasn't a fishing boat and you know it. It had a black flag and besides who calls a fishing boat the *Black Skull*?"

"Said, you. I never saw any name. For all I know, it was called the *Titanic*."

"Fine, whatever, go look at fish traps. I'm going to find a pirate ship." Murphy headed toward the back of the building.

Those fish traps are pretty amazing.

He walked on and paused at the gold mining display. He was captivated by the stories of men who had risked it all to go to the Klondike. It was fascinating to him how some men had removed a few yards of overburden and become instant millionaires and others had toiled a lifetime and died poor.

He approached the shipping exhibit and looked through the various displays depicting the many shipwrecks in Southeast Alaska. He searched for any mention of pirates, reading every placard and every newspaper article. Murphy studied the many pictures and connecting stories detailing wrecks and the daring rescues that took place in the dangerous waters around Douglas and Juneau. When his search was exhausted, he'd found no mention of pirates or a ship called the *Black Skull*.

He gave up and went to find Katrina. He quickly spotted her bright pink hair. She was studying the intricate weaving of an ancient tapestry. He tapped her on her right shoulder, then jumped to the left.

Katrina glanced right then left. "Real mature."

"What are you looking at?" He asked.

She pointed at a yellow, black and white blanket or robe. Its intricate designs featured traditional Tlingit images of the wolf and the raven.

"It says this Chilkat chief's robe is over two hundred years old, pretty cool, huh?" She gestured at the robe.

"It was woven by Tlingit women, out of mountain goat and dog hair over two centuries ago." She gazed down at her pre-ripped jeans. "None of my clothes will last twenty years." She shook her head and returned her eyes to the masterpiece.

"Huh? Dog hair? I wonder what it smells like when it's wet." Murphy smirked.

"This is some of the finest weaving in the history of the world and that's what you get from it? You wonder what it smells like wet?" She spoke in a slow caveman drawl, turning her back to him to block his view of the tapestry as if to say he wasn't worthy of seeing it.

Murphy shrugged and grinned.

Katrina turned away from the robe and asked, "Well, did you find the USS *Jolly Roger Skull* whatever thingy?"

"No, there's nothing about the *Black Skull* but let's go ask Mrs. Sutter." He turned and walked away.

Katrina followed. "All right, let's get this over with."

Mrs. Sutter's office was in the far-right corner of the building. Her office door was wide open and Murphy rapped lightly on the door jamb. He felt positive she would be helpful in his quest.

Chapter 6: Mrs. Sutter

Mrs. Sutter sat on an antique captain's chair behind a great oak desk in the rear of the large room beneath a small window. A single ray of sunshine pierced the glass pane illuminating her snow-white hair.

She looked up from a scattered pile of papers and gestured for them to come in. Her hair was kept in a tight bun; half-round glasses perched on her long thin nose. She studied them with piercing gray eyes. Her face was pinched as though she'd recently eaten a lemon. She was partly hidden behind high stacks of books, papers, animal bones, mineral samples, and numerous unidentifiable antiquities.

Murphy's eyes were immediately drawn to a small cannon in the center of the great desk. "Is that real?"

Mrs. Sutter peered over the top of her glasses directly into Murphy's eyes. "Young man, is what real?"

"That cannon, it's super fly." He reached toward it but thought better and stuffed his hand in his pocket.

Mrs. Sutter smiled. "Hello, Murphy. Hello, Katrina."

"Hello, Mrs. Sutter," they answered in unison.

"I love your hair, Katrina. And yes, young man, the cannon is real."

"Does it work?" Murphy asked.

"Thank you." Katrina responded.

"Yes, it does work. The Coast Guard lent it to us for a display we are working on to honor their history in Alaska. They use it for ceremonies mostly, but it will shoot out a projectile."

"Wow! That's so cool."

"I agree. It is cool. It usually catches everyone's eye." She gestured toward two chairs. "Why don't you two take a seat and tell me what brings you to my desk on such a beautiful day." Mrs. Sutter produced a coffee-stained porcelain mug from somewhere in the clutter and took a quick sip.

After they were seated, Murphy immediately told her what they had seen.

When he finished, Mrs. Sutter was quiet for a moment. Then she slowly pushed herself back a few inches from her desk. She looked at Murphy, then Katrina, and back to Murphy.

"That's quite a tale you've spun, Murphy."

She looked at Katrina. "You saw all this, too?"

Katrina took a quick side glance at Murphy.

"Kinda, I guess. I mean, I saw some old wrecked fishing boat and some men. I didn't see a flag or scary name or cutlasses or a cannon or Purple Beard or bloody skulls."

"*Black Skull.*" Murphy muttered.

"So, no pirates for you, hey?" Mrs. Sutter asked Katrina.

"There was definitely something shady with those men and that boat, but pirates here, now, come on that seems a bit crazy to me. Sorry, Murphy, but maybe you wanted to see a pirate ship more than I did."

"They were digging for treasure, fishermen don't do that." He exclaimed.

"What do you mean digging for treasure? Did you see them digging?" Mrs. Sutter queried.

"No, ma'am. But my mom told me about people finding freshly dug holes in their yard. It must be the pirates. Probably looking for lost treasure."

Mrs. Sutter looked toward Katrina.

Katrina shook her head. "First I've heard of this."

"Mom said Mrs. Jones, our neighbor, found holes in her back yard the day after we saw the *Black Skull.*"

"That is very interesting, Murphy."

"What part, Mrs. Sutter?" he asked.

"That name. Mr. Carlson was searching for something called, *Black Skull.*"

Murphy immediately straightened up and scooted to the edge of his chair.

"I heard him mention it on the phone one time. He said to someone on the other end of the line, 'Hey, boss. I've got some info on the *Black Skull.*' He seemed very excited." Mrs. Sutter twisted in her chair and pointed. "See those air registers on the floor?"

Murphy and Katrina turned in their chairs and saw a number of ornate cast iron grills.

Mrs. Sutter pointed to one directly behind her desk. "See that one? It lets in more than air. If you're near it downstairs, I can hear whatever you say. Everyone knows this but Mr. Carlson apparently." She winked conspiratorially.

"All he ever did was hang out in the basement, rummage through the donations we receive regularly and search the archives. I asked if I could help him search one time but he turned me down and never said what it was that consumed all his time." She pulled a tissue from a box hidden somewhere in the clutter on her desk and briefly blew her nose.

Murphy was impressed when she balled it up and without looking tossed it over her shoulder where it landed neatly in the center of a small waste basket that sat in the corner behind her chair.

"Nobody cared for him much. He was an odd bird, that one."

"Who is he? Who's Mr. Carlson?" Katrina asked.

"Oh, he was our most recent museum curator. He took the job after Mrs. Smith passed away last year."

"Was? Did he quit?" Murphy asked.

"Yes, he did, a little over a month ago. I came in one Saturday and found a note on my desk saying there had been a family tragedy and he was resigning immediately."

The lights flickered off and back on. They all glanced up at the overhead light.

Mrs. Sutter looked at an enormous round oak clock on the wall. It was twelve noon. A placard under the clock read, "This once hung on the wall of the Alaska Juneau Mining Company's main office."

"Oh, how the time flies. It's noon already. If you didn't see the notice on the door, we are closing today at one o'clock. Our floor wax machine has been repaired and Mike Marshal is waxing now. You know him; he does the floors at your school as well. It's the last weekend before the first cruise ships start showing up. After that, there won't be time until fall." Mrs. Sutter tidied a jumble of papers on her desk as she talked.

"We didn't see it." Murphy and Katrina said at the same time.

"Well, you have an hour before I have to kick you out."

"So, you think Mr. Carlson was searching for information about a ship called the *Black Skull?*" Murphy asked.

"Until you told me your story, I had no idea what it was. It only stuck in my head because it sounded unusual and Carlson seemed so obsessed with finding something. I assumed that's what it was, information about something called the *Black Skull.*"

"Did you ever see him again?" Katrina flipped pink strands of hair out of her face.

"No, we thought he left town but my husband saw him talking to Ned Fisher at the boat harbor the other day. Maybe he's back or he never left, who knows with that one?"

"I called Mr. Fisher about the *Black Skull*. He's pretty smart about boat and ship history around here, but he'd never heard of any ship or boat named *Black Skull*."

"Hmmm, yes, Ned is a knowledgeable historian, for sure." She retrieved her stained mug and took a swallow.

"Carlson's never come back here as far as I know, but he didn't leave his keys, and Arnie Boyko, our volunteer coordinator, swears items have been moved around in our storage area downstairs." Mrs. Sutter shoved her glasses up her nose. "He's convinced Carlson is sneaking around here at night. Between you and me, Arnie also thinks the place is haunted so you can take what he says with a grain of salt."

Murphy was quiet for a minute. "I sure wish I knew what he found."

Mrs. Sutter glanced at the big clock. "I'll tell you what, you have most of an hour before we close. Mr. Carlson kept a small office in the basement."

She pulled another tissue from somewhere in the center of the jumbled desk and briefly blew her nose. Again, she nailed the no-look shot and the balled-up tissue landed neatly in the center of the waste basket.

"No one has touched it since he left. It's a complete mess, chock full of letters, books, charts and who knows what, but if you two want to dig through it you can. But be careful, some of it is delicate and any of it could be an important piece of history."

"Really? Yes, ma'am. We'll be careful. Right, Kat?"

Katrina smiled. "Yay, digging through junk, my fav."

Mrs. Sutter rose from her desk. She was tall and lean and Murphy noticed she wore hiking boots. Thick wool socks were folded neatly over the tops.

"Come on, I'll take you downstairs."

They followed her out of her office to the other side of the building and down a narrow dimly-lit staircase. Reaching the lower floor, Murphy and Katrina were amazed to see a virtual sea of books, paperwork, antiques, and artifacts. Some of it appeared to be organized on shelves, but much was haphazardly stacked or piled randomly across the large open room.

"It looks like a maze." Katrina observed.

Mrs. Sutter led them through with a practiced ease. They promptly arrived at a small office in the rear of the enormous room. It was the only other room in the basement aside from two small enclosures under the stairwell.

Murphy read a small sign beside the door of the tiny office: *D.L. Carlson, Curator.*

Mrs. Sutter pulled open the door and stood aside. "Have at it and good luck."

They cautiously entered the tiny windowless office. At first glance, Murphy noticed every flat surface was covered with papers, pamphlets, books, and nautical charts. There was barely room to move through the stacks of cardboard boxes on the floor.

"I hope you solve your mystery, Murphy. I have to go to an appointment so I'll let Mike know you are down here. Keep an eye on the clock. I'm glad you came by. Katrina, say hi to your dad."

"Okay, I will."

"And Murphy, please say hi to your mom for me." Mrs. Sutter disappeared into the maze of antiquities. Her footsteps retreated up the stairwell.

Katrina looked at Murphy. "What was that about?"

He shrugged. "What?"

"Your dad, why didn't she ask you to say hi to him?"

"Oh, that's a long story."

"I've got time."

"My mom says she harbors a grievance against my dad. I'll tell you about it later. We don't have much time, let's look for clues."

"That's suspicious. What did he do?"

"Mom said he ruined her world."

"What? That's epic. How?"

Murphy moved toward the desk.

"Hey you can't leave me hanging."

"I promise I'll tell you the whole story after we leave, but help me search first. Please."

"Okay, but you better."

"I will, I will. Hurry, start looking, we don't have much time."

Chapter 7: Searching

Murphy removed a stack of books from the plain four-legged office chair. He sat down at the small crowded desk. He observed the desk had a wide center drawer and three deeper, narrower drawers on the right side.

Katrina approached a stack of boxes in the corner. "What exactly am I looking for?"

"Anything that says *Black Skull* or pirates or Alaska shipwrecks."

"Okay I've got it, anything about Captain Hook or the *Titanic*."

"Funny."

Murphy pulled open the center drawer in the desk. It was full of the usual things in desk drawers. Pencils, pens, paperclips, a stapler and a letter opener. There wasn't anything of interest to him so he closed it and pulled open the top drawer on the right side of the desk. Inside he found a thick bundle of envelopes bound with a wide rubber band. He removed the rubber band, stretched it around his index finger and his thumb, then pointed it at Katrina.

Her head stayed still but her eyes followed him.

"You do, you're dead." She said menacingly.

He grinned sheepishly and shot the rubber band across the room. He lifted out half of the stack of letters and set them on the desk.

"Hey, here's a book on shipwrecks in Alaska, now what?" Katrina called from the corner.

He turned his chair to face her. She was holding a large book with a glossy cover.

"Can you look in the index and see if *Black Skull* is mentioned?"

He turned back and grabbed the first letter on the stack and scanned it quickly. It was a letter to a fisherman from his wife. No pirate ships. Murphy scanned letter after letter and Katrina continued searching through boxes of books.

"Hey, this might actually be something." She was sitting on the floor surrounded by stacks of books and empty boxes. He saw she was holding a paperback book. It was approximately the same size as a National Geographic magazine, but thinner. She had it open and was reading a page. He could see it was typewritten.

"What does it say, Kat?"

"It says this ... I guess it's a magazine," she turned it over in her hand. "It's a bunch of unpublished newspaper stories a guy named Albert Romer put together himself. It says he was a reporter for the *Juneau Empire* like a thousand years ago or something."

"Okay. What does he say about the *Black Skull*?"

"Nothing."

"Nothing? What are you talking about then?"

"Chillax, I'm getting to it. Let me read it."

Murphy heaved a sigh and sat back in his chair. He knew from past experience he shouldn't try to hurry her.

"So, this guy Albert Romer wrote about some boat called the *Finch*. That's a funny name. Anyway, it hit a rock and sank on Douglas Island one night during a bad storm. He says it had a lot of gold on it from the Klondike gold rush. Why does it have MV in front of its name?"

"It means marine vessel," he answered. "Something I learned from doing models."

Katrina ignored his dig and tilted the booklet to the light. "It says seven people died including the captain who went down with his ship. That's a real thing? I thought it was a saying."

"It was a real thing back in the day, like when there were pirates." He grinned.

"This Albert dude says he interviewed a survivor of the wreck after fishermen pulled him from the water. He said he saw a pirate ship dangerously close to the *Finch* before they hit the rocks. He thinks they were pushed into the rocks by this ship."

"What does he say it was called? Did it have a black flag?"

"Doesn't say. The article was never printed. This Romer guy says it's because his editor thought the survivor was delirious with hypothermia. And Romer agreed."

"Let me see." Murphy reached out and Katrina handed him the booklet. He scanned the page but quickly realized there wasn't anything more. "This does prove there might have been pirates around here though."

Katrina looked up at him and smirked. "Does it?"

"Keep looking."

He picked up another envelope and fished out the next letter. It turned out to be a grievance letter to an engineer on the SS *Sophia* sent from headquarters in Victoria, British Columbia. Apparently on a recent visit to Juneau the engineer had acted in a manner unbefitting an employee of the shipping company. Murphy was finishing the last page when Katrina spoke.

"This journal is cool."

He turned to see her holding a leather-bound diary or journal. The bronzed leather was cracked and pealing, the pages were stained brown and yellow and were severely crinkled. Murphy sniffed the air. "It smells moldy."

"It's not the only thing that smells moldy around here."

"Mold is gold."

"What?"

"Nothing, it's something my dad always says."

She opened the journal and read out loud. "Property of First mate Lawrence Corbin II. SS *Islander*. Why do they all have letters in front of their names?"

"They who?"

"Ships, they all have letters in front of their names."

"Oh, they mean stuff like MV is marine vessel, SS is steamship."

"Let me guess, you learned that from building models?" She ribbed.

"Actually, I learned it from my dad." He paused a beat. "While building models."

"I knew it. Hey, so FV is fishing vessel. I just figured that out." She smiled.

"Only after having a dad who has been a commercial fisherman most of your life."

"Whatever."

She turned her attention to the journal, flipping to the first page while holding it so they could both see.

They saw dates and entries written in precise neat handwriting. The ink was faded but legible. Katrina flipped to the next page and the next, then used her thumb to flip faster. She stopped and went back a few pages.

Murphy watched her but picked up a handful of letters.

Katrina spoke up. "The last entry is circled in black marker. They didn't have those when Mr. Corbin was writing in his journal."

"What does it say?"

"It's dated August 16, 1901."

> Our departure and voyage south down
> Lynn Canal were initially routine. Weather
> was overcast with 20 naught fore winds.
> I pulled ice watch, the midnight to three
> AM shift. Between scans of the horizon for
> burgs I entered yesterday's events.

Katrina flipped back a page and scanned the entry. "Yup, this one is all about being in Skagway and loading cargo, but it's dated the fourteenth, there's nothing for the fifteenth."

She turned the page back to the circled entry.

> Wind picked up around one AM. The
> sky was heavily overcast and brooding, the
> waves and spray made visibility difficult.
> I sighted a burg off our port side at 1:50
> AM. I sounded the proper claxon, alerting
> the bridge. At 1:54 AM I was thrown to the
> deck by an unexpected jolt. The burg was
> still 20 fathoms off our port bow. As I got
> to my feet, I glimpsed a looming shadow to
> our starboard side.

Katrina absently tucked an unruly lock of fuchsia hair behind her ear as she was reading.

> It was a smaller vessel, completely
> darkened, not running any lights at all.
> It appeared to me, the smaller vessel was
> shoving us into the burg.

"That's them, that's got to be the pirates he's talking about." Murphy was excited.

"Let me finish, Captain Murphy Beard."

"Great, you heard that, too?"

"Yes, I did and it's extra funny, now let me finish."

"Please do." He scooched to the edge of his chair.

> I'm not certain of the time but I'll
> approximate it was 2:00 AM when we
> struck the burg. I was thrown overboard
> and eventually picked up by a boat and

brought to shore. With many others, I lost
everything but my life and this journal. I
consider myself one of the lucky ones.

"Does he write anything more about the *Black Skull*?"

"He didn't say it was the *Black Skull*."

After attempts to relay what I saw to
other surviving crew members I was
completely ignored. No one else reported
seeing a ship in the vicinity. After one
comment suggesting I was drinking on
watch, and it might be my fault we hit the
burg, I've decided this is the last time I'll
discuss this matter verbally or in writing.

"That's it, last entry." She closed the small journal and tossed it on a nearby stack of books.

"Not everything I was hoping for, but that's more evidence of piracy around here." He squirmed excitedly in the chair. He held a thick envelope in his right hand as he spoke. It was yellow with age and worn at the corners.

"Check this out." He waved it in the air. "It's addressed, and looks like it was sealed. Someone cut it open. It's never been mailed, there's no post marks. That's pretty weird."

A low vibration started in the floor and quickly intensified. The books on the shelves began to tremble, the single hanging light bulb flickered. Pencils and pens in a mason jar on the desk rattled. The half open office door slammed shut with a jarring crash.

They were startled. Murphy bolted upright from the chair.

"Oh, my gosh." Katrina leapt to her feet. "Was that another quake?"

Murphy glanced at his watch. "Uh-oh. We're way late. We should have been out of here an hour ago. Mr. Marshal must be doing the floors and forgot about us, or Mrs. Sutter forgot to tell him we were down here. She was in a hurry."

Katrina twisted the door knob and pushed. It didn't move. She put her shoulder to it and pushed harder. The door remained stuck. "Help me."

The drone of the floor waxer filled the air. Murphy moved to the door and shoved.

"Let's push at the same time. One, two, three, go."

They both pushed mightily. The door didn't budge. They were trapped.

Chapter 8: Trapped

Katrina banged on the door with her fist. "Hey! Help! Let us out!"

"I don't think anyone will hear you with all that noise." Murphy looked at the ceiling. "And the only one in the whole building besides us is Mr. Marshal and he def can't hear us."

Stacks of papers continued to rustle on the shelves. The pens and pencils jangled to a random beat in the glass on the desk.

"Well, what are we going to do?" Katrina asked.

"You have a phone, call your dad."

"He's a hundred miles off shore." She fished a smart phone out of her back pocket.

"Oh, yeah, duh. I forgot."

She tapped the screen a couple of times and handed it to Murphy. "You call your dad."

"He's at a conference in Anchorage. I'll call Mom." He reminded her.

Murphy tapped in his mom's cell number and held the phone to his ear. After a moment, he pulled it away and looked at the screen. "Nothing, it's not ringing. There's no bars." He glanced about. "We're in a concrete basement. Underground. I don't think we're getting reception." He handed back the phone.

Katrina held it above her head and moved about the room. She soon shook her head. "Nothing." She shoved the phone back in her pocket.

Murphy glanced about the small enclosure. "Maybe there's a phone in here."

Katrina turned in a slow circle. "You mean a land line? I guess a museum is the right place for one."

A quick search proved futile, there wasn't even a place to plug a phone in.

Murphy looked up. "Maybe if we can bang on the ceiling, Mr. Marshal will hear us. Do you see a broom or mop?"

"No, it's not the custodian's closet. This is the curator's office."

Murphy cleared some space on the desk and hopped up on to it. He reached toward the ceiling but it was too high and he was a yard short. "Help me stack up a couple boxes."

Katrina stood up and grabbed a box off of a nearby stack. They quickly had a stairway of sorts built from six boxes.

"Here goes." Murphy stepped onto the first box.

"Be careful."

"Don't worry. I won't fall." He took another step up.

"I was talking about the books, don't hurt them."

He took the third and last step. He reached up and grasped a sprinkler pipe with one hand, made a fist with the other and banged on the ceiling. His fists barely made a sound on the thick concrete floor.

He shook his hand. "Ow! That's not going to work, the floor is too thick. Even if I had a hammer, he'd never hear it."

Katrina pointed at a grill in the ceiling to Murphy's right. "Is that the vent Mrs. Sutter was talking about?"

Murphy looked. He recognized it was one of the ornate floor grills Mrs. Sutter had pointed out in her office.

He jumped down. "Help me move the desk over. I'll yell though the vent. Mr. Marshal should hear that."

They cleared a path and struggled to drag the desk into position under the floor grill. Once in place, they quickly rebuilt their makeshift staircase. Murphy carefully climbed up. He got his mouth as close to the vent as he could.

"Hello, hello, Mr. Marshal, can you hear me? Hello. Hello."

He tried again and again. Katrina yelled, too.

"Hello. Hey, Mr. Marshal! Help us, let us out!"

Eventually Murphy climbed down. "He's never going to hear us. All we can do is hope he takes a break and turns that stupid waxer off."

He sat on the corner of the desk. He noticed a smudge of dirt on his knee below his khaki shorts. He licked a finger and rubbed it away.

Katrina stood under the vent in the ceiling and stared up at it. "I can fit through that."

"What?" Murphy looked at the grill. "No way."

'I'll bet you."

"I don't want to bet, but if you think you can, let's see it."

"Fine."

She nimbly hopped on to the desk and scurried up the box staircase. She grabbed the sprinkler pipe with both hands and swung her legs over the pipe. Hanging from only her legs, she reached out with both hands and grabbed the grate. She pulled and wrenched at it.

"I need something to pry with."

Murphy remembered seeing the letter opener and retrieved it from the top desk drawer. He handed it up to her.

Katrina wedged the point of the silver letter opener in the crack around the edge of the grill. She pried and the grate moved slightly. She began working the letter opener around the edge much like opening a paint can. Within a few seconds, she yelled, "Look out!" The grate fell to the floor with a clatter.

Katrina reached into the opening. Most of her arm disappeared into the ceiling.

"I can reach the top grate but my arm isn't long enough to push up."

"Here use this." Murphy handed up a tightly-rolled nautical chart. It had a rubber band around each end. Katrina grabbed it and used it to push up the top grate.

The vibration and loud hum of the waxer continued.

"I still don't think you'll fit."

"Are you calling me fat?'

Murphy's checks reddened. "No, I'm just … I mean, it's a small hole."

She smiled at his discomfort, and with a flurry of motion dropped her legs and hung from only her hands. "Move those boxes."

Murphy quickly removed the boxes from the desk and got out of her way as she began swinging back and forth like a pendulum. She quickly gained momentum and swung her body as she shifted her grip slightly on the pipe, aligning herself directly with the opening in the ceiling. With a final swing, she pointed her toes and shot up into the opening feet first. In a second, she had completely disappeared.

Murphy stared at the hole. His mouth slowly opened. "Cool," he said to the empty room.

Within a minute, he heard a commotion at the office door. He called out. "Katrina?"

"Yeah, it's me." Her voice was muffled. "Hold on I have to move some boxes."

He listened at the door as he heard her work. Suddenly the knob turned and the door was flung wide.

Katrina bowed and said, "Ta da!"

"That was pretty awesome."

"I know."

"Did you see Mr. Marshal up there?"

"No, he was up in the front. I just ran down here first."

"Thank you."

"You're welcome."

She began restacking boxes with Murphy's help.

Murphy said. "Kind of strange that the vibration caused only this stack of boxes to fall over."

Katrina looked around the room. "It is pretty sus it blocked the door, conveniently trapping us in. I think it was on purpose. Someone pushed it. But who?"

"You think it was Mr. Marshal?" he glanced at the ceiling.

"The door slammed right after the vibration started. No way he did both. Okay, it was Arnie Boyko's ghosts or Mr. Carlson, the creepy curator. Either way something weird is going on. I'm out of here." She turned toward the stairway.

They hurried through the maze of boxes and ran up the flight of steps. They saw Mr. Marshal on the opposite side of the museum. He was wearing navy blue coveralls and had a pair of bright red headphones squished down over his bushy head of hair. He was dancing behind the waxer and singing off key above the incessant drone of the machine.

Murphy and Katrina looked at each other. She shook her head, he shrugged and they turned toward the exit.

Katrina buckled her helmet strap as Murphy unzipped his backpack. The sky had darkened and there was a fine mist in the air. He wanted his jacket for the ride home.

"What's that?" Katrina asked.

"What's what?"

"In your hand."

Murphy looked down and saw he was still holding the unmailed letter.

Chapter 9: Murderer's Tale

Murphy and Katrina made it home in time for supper. Before telling Murphy's mom what happened to them, they'd agreed to leave out the part about accidentally stealing a letter from the city museum. They decided they'd go together to return it to Mrs. Sutter the following Saturday.

Murphy was slightly miffed after telling his mom about the clues they had found, being trapped in the cluttered office and their eventual escape. She had laughed, high fived Katrina and shouted, "Girl Power!"

He went to his room to read the letter.

When he emerged sometime later, he was excited. He was clutching the pages of the letter tightly in his hand. He plopped down on the brown suede couch opposite the matching love seat where Katrina was sitting and writing in her diary. She had her ear buds in and was tapping her foot to a beat. Murphy waved the pages at her and she slowly removed the ear buds.

"Let me guess. That letter is from a pirate."

"No, but, yeah, well, kind of. Listen and I'll tell you."

Katrina swung her legs to the floor and sat with her elbows on her knees as if she was settling in for a long wait. Murphy couldn't help but notice her rainbow-colored toe socks.

Hogan came in from the kitchen where he had undoubtedly been on crumb patrol, a responsibility he took seriously. He licked Murphy's hand and managed to get one slobbery lap across his face before being pushed away.

"Get down, Hoge." Murphy wiped his face with the sleeve of his shirt. "Yuck, dog food."

Hogan curled into a ball at his feet.

Katrina observed it all with a look of disinterest. "You two done?"

"Okay, so this letter?" Murphy shook it in his hand. "It's from a lady who lived in Juneau a long time ago. Her name was Gretta Smythe and she wrote it to her sister in Kansas in 1903 but never sent it."

"Like that's not weird at all." Katrina spoke.

"Yes, but I think I know why she didn't send it."

"Let's hear your deductions, Mr. Holmes, sir."

Murphy smiled. "That would make you Watson."

"Yeah, no. Anyway, what does it say?"

He glanced at the pages in his hand. "This Gretta lady was a court reporter and she wrote to her sister about a trial she worked. She explained the entire trial in this letter but for some reason she never sent it. She wrote to her sister that she took an oath to not discuss the case, but the grizzly details were gnawing away at her. Gretta felt the need to tell someone."

"What was it about? The trial, I mean?"

"It was a murder trial. This guy named Blackwell, he was a member of a gang of thieves and murderers. He was on trial for killing one of his own gang members, a guy named Larson."

Katrina sat up straight. "Wow, Juneau was the wild west back in the day."

"It says he stabbed him in the heart. That's pretty brutal."

Murphy jabbed his finger toward her. "So, the Blackwell dude pleaded guilty and refused to let the court-appointed lawyer defend him. He said he was guilty and deserved to die for his crimes."

Katrina pointed her finger at her head and did a circling motion.

"But he wasn't crazy. He also wouldn't allow the lawyer to enter a plea of insanity. If he had and it worked, it would have saved him from being hanged. I think he wanted to die."

Katrina's eyes grew larger. "Hanged? They hung people in Juneau? Hanged, I mean? No way!"

"Way! That's how they did it back then."

"I guess I thought that only happened in Texas, in the old west."

"Juneau was the old west too, old North West."

"What does any of this have to do with your pirates?"

"I'm getting to that. Larson and Blackwell knew each other from Seattle where they worked mostly as fishermen. They thought they could come to Juneau and strike it rich in the gold mines." Murphy was momentarily distracted by the neighbor's dog barking and the low drone from the TV in his parents' room.

Hogan looked up, cocked his head and gave a short woof.

"Hoge, be quiet." Murphy admonished.

"After working in the mines awhile, they figured they would never get rich. And having spent their lives at sea they hated being underground. So, they came up with a crazy plan."

"They stole gold from the mine," Katrina blurted.

"Not from the mine."

"Ah ha, they did steal gold." She put her hand up to high five.

Murphy absently smacked her palm. "They did steal gold but they stole it from ships."

"Ships? How?"

"That's the good part. They built a fake pirate ship, black flag and all, then they pushed or tricked ships into hitting rocks or ice burgs."

Katrina's posture stiffened. "No way!"

"Way. They also moved marker buoys and knocked out lighthouse lights. Larson and Blackwell added some more guys to the gang, mostly other men from the mines. The plan was to be close enough to a stricken ship for the thieves to board and steal gold."

"Seems a bit sketchy to me. Why didn't they get noticed?"

Murphy gestured with the letter. "The letter says Blackwell told the court that during the panic no one noticed a few extra men running around. He said they paid a man in the harbormaster's office in Skagway to tell them which ships were carrying gold from the Klondike. He told them their schedules and even in which cabins the richest passengers were berthed."

Murphy looked over Katrina's shoulder out the window at the lights of downtown Juneau shimmering on the surface of the channel.

"Why did one guy kill the other guy?" she asked.

"The Blackwell guy told the court they got rich fast, but reporters and police were getting curious about rumors of pirate ship sightings. Larson and Blackwell buried the gold and decided they would wait a year to dig it up and divide it."

"Where? Where did they bury it? Are we rich?"

"The murderer, Blackwell, swore to take the secret to his grave."

"Bummer, where did they hide their ship?"

"I forgot that part. They kept it hidden in a small lagoon on an island not far from Juneau, reachable only at high tide. They burned it. The ship, I mean."

"Why? Why did they burn it?"

"They were scared they were about to be busted. They'd killed people and they knew they would be hanged if caught. So they burned the fake pirate ship and went back to work in the mines until things cooled off."

Murphy heard more barking from Fluffy. Hogan raised his head. Murphy scratched his ears and he lay back down.

"Get back to why did one bad guy stab the other bad guy in the heart?" Katrina urged.

"Well, after they all got real jobs, the other three members of the gang were killed in a cave-in at the Treadwell Mine. Larson wanted his half right away and Blackwell wanted to wait. They fought and Blackwell stabbed Larson."

"What happened to the gold?"

"I don't think it was ever found, at least it didn't say in the letter."

Katrina smoothed her bangs with her fingers. "I still don't buy that some suspicious dudes could sail around in a fake pirate ship and no one ever saw them."

"The letter says the gang only attacked at night or during bad storms."

"Okay. What about where they hid their ship? How could it be hidden close to Juneau and never be seen?"

"The Blackwell dude said it was an area with lots of reefs and swift currents and boats normally stayed clear of it."

"Answers for everything, huh? So, what happened?"

"What? Oh, to Blackwell? Gretta Smythe's letter said that he got the death sentence and two weeks later he was hanged at the Juneau Jail."

"This would be a great movie. I'll write the script." She waved the pen she had been using in the air.

Murphy paused. He could hear a rhythmic thumping accompanying the drone of the TV in his parents' room. It was the familiar sound of his mom running on the treadmill. He was lost in thought, but he snapped out of it, suddenly energized, and waved the pages in the air. "I haven't told you the best part."

Katrina was staring at the wall and didn't seem to notice him.

Probably writing her script in her head.

He stopped talking but continued to stare at her. Eventually, she noticed him gawking and her eyes focused on his face. He was smiling.

"What—what!" She demanded.

"There's more and it's the best part." He squirmed a little. The smile didn't leave his face.

"You said no one knew where the gold was. Do you?"

"No, it's not that, it's even better."

"What could be better than finding stolen pirate gold?"

"Okay maybe not better but it's the coolest thing ever."

"What then?"

"The name of the fake pirate ship."

Katrina dropped her pen and sat up straight. "No freaking way, you lie! Is any of what you just said true?"

"It's all in the letter, including the name of the gang's ship."

"No way."

"Way. It was the *Black Skull*." Murphy shot up from the couch and did a quick version of the Carlton dance he'd learned from an old rerun sitcom his dad watched.

Katrina stood up, too. "Let me see the letter," she demanded.

Murphy quickly shuffled the pages and handed one to Katrina. He stabbed at the page with his finger. "Right there. *Black Skull*."

Katrina took the page and scanned it.

He looked over her shoulder. Hogan moved to a heat vent behind the couch and stretched out like a cat.

After a moment, Katrina lowered the page. "This is off the hook; you were kind of right."

"Kind of!" He was indignant. "What do you mean, kind of? This proves," he shook the pages, "there is a pirate ship called the *Black Skull*."

"It proves there was a pirate ship, well a fake one, called the *Black Skull*." Katrina answered. "If this Gretta lady is even telling the truth."

"Come on, this is proof." He shook the pages that were clutched fiercely in his fist.

"But it doesn't explain how we saw a ship that was supposedly destroyed lifetimes ago right out there." She pointed to the channel. "Only a few days ago."

"People keep telling me that." He answered.

She sat down on the love seat. "I do have to admit something fishy is going on."

Murphy sat down opposite her. "I don't understand it either, but we did see it, so it's real, and the letter proves it."

She yawned. "Your dad will be back tomorrow. Maybe he knows something about the trial."

"I saw a book in his shop one time called *Mysteries and Murders in Alaska's Capital*. I grabbed it up because it had the Bird Man of Alcatraz on the cover. He did his first murder in Juneau."

"Who?"

"The Bird Man of Alcatraz, it's a long story. Search him." He yawned. "I'm going to bed. See you in the morning."

"Wait a minute. Speaking of your dad, you never told me why Mrs. Sutter and him have a beef."

"I'll have my dad tell you when he gets back. I promise, but not now. I'm too tired." He headed down the hallway toward his room. Hogan followed close behind, licking his hand before he could pull it away.

"Hogan!"

Chapter 10: Second Opinion

Murphy's dad arrived in the early morning. They enjoyed a big family breakfast, as his dad liked to call it. Murphy and Katrina were in charge of the pancakes, Sonia handled the eggs and John fried the bacon. Hogan chased crumbs.

After the dishes and the kitchen were cleaned, Katrina put in her earbuds and headed to the living room. Sonia attended a virtual meeting for work in her office. Murphy and his dad stayed at the breakfast bar. His dad wore a Hawaiian style shirt covered in pink and blue parrots and tan cargo shorts with black tube socks pulled all the way to his thick pale knees. They called it his cruise ship chic look.

Murphy filled him in on his conversation with Mr. Fisher and their trip to the museum, including what he had discovered in the letter written by Gretta Smythe.

John pulled his reading glasses from his shirt pocket, took the pages from Murphy and began reading.

Murphy watched as his dad's his brow furrowed deeper and deeper as he read. "This proves Katrina and I saw a pirate ship. Right, Dad?"

John adjusted his glasses but didn't answer.

"Dad, are you listening?"

John looked up and stared at his son for a long second. "Of course, I'm listening. Ned Fisher, the museum, Katrina's escape, this letter."

"Our escape." Murphy muttered.

"What's that, son?"

Murphy didn't answer but asked a question instead. "In all your books and papers, have you ever heard of the Blackwell-Larson case?" He retrieved an orange from a bowl on the counter and began to peal it.

The drone of a neighbor's lawnmower was punctuated by a loud metallic clang and immediately followed be a bellowed curse. John glanced at Murphy as the edges of his mouth fluttered and his eyes sparkled.

Murphy noticed and grinned from ear to ear.

John raised his eyebrows and looked down his nose at his son.

Murphy's face immediately went deadpan, but he couldn't hide the mischievous glint in his eyes. He finished peeling the orange and laid the intact peel on the counter. It resembled the head of an African elephant. Hogan was inconveniently and uncomfortably crammed under his stool. He was on his back, head resting on a rung and all four white feet flopping in the air as he dreamed. The steady hum of Mr. Wallace's lawnmower was continually interrupted by loud clangs and louder curses.

"What I do know," John began answering Murphy's question. "The case isn't in any books or papers I've come across. I know of three separate books written about sensational trials in Juneau's past. I've read them all and there is nothing about a Blackwell or a Larson that I can remember."

Murphy hopped off of his stool, moved to the sink and rinsed his hands. Hogan squiggled out from under the stool, almost toppling it in his haste. He managed to slather one of Murphy's hands with his tongue before it was pulled away.

"Great, so old Gretta Smythe was looney toons then?" Murphy dried his hands on a dish towel.

"Maybe, maybe not."

Murphy retook his stool and looked quizzically at his dad.

John continued. "So, the date on the letter was two years after the sinking of the SS *Islander*. A year after that the courthouse was burned by an unknown arsonist."

He removed his reading glasses and rubbed his eyes. "All current case files were destroyed. I'm guessing if cases were sealed, they were lost forever."

Murphy sat up straighter. "Why do you think she didn't send the letter?"

"We'll never know for sure, but people died young back then from all sorts of ailments easily cured today. There weren't even flu shots."

Clang!

Murphy covered his ears. His dad nodded and smiled.

John set the pages on the bar. "This letter mentions Blackwell had a court appointed lawyer. There was only one documented court appointed defense lawyer in Juneau during that time. A Mr. Gerald W. Florence, Esquire. He would have worked the Blackwell case."

After their conversation, John pulled a book off a shelf and handed it to Murphy. It was titled *Defending the Rogues of Alaska: A Biography on the Life of Gerald W. Florence, Esquire.*

★ ★ ★

Murphy spent the evening on his bean bag chair pouring through the book. He learned that Mr. Florence was quite the celebrity in his middle years. He'd moved on from public service to the private sector and defended some of Alaska's most notorious criminals. He practiced well into his eighties often taking cases pro bono in the later part of his career.

Murphy walked into the living room to put the book back on the shelf. He heard a noise in the kitchen. When he entered, Katrina was standing at the bar in her bare feet. She had a silver toe ring on each of her pinkies. She was swaying back and forth and Murphy could hear the music blaring from her earbuds. She was doing a crossword puzzle in pen.

When she noticed Murphy, she yelled, "What's an eleven-letter word for gizzard?"

Murphy was startled and visibly jolted backwards.

Katrina noticed and pulled out an ear bud. "Oops, was I loud?"

Murphy tilted his head and faked smacking one ear. "What? Can't hear you."

"Funny"

"Thank you. Hey, do you want to check out some old dead lawyer dude's house after the museum on Saturday?"

Katrina clutched her heart and batted her eye lids. "You had me at old dead lawyer."

"Weirdo. Anyway, Mr. Florence—"

Katrina cut him off. "The old dead lawyer?"

Murphy looked exasperated but continued. "Yes, him. He died in 1979, that's the dead part, at his house and it's still there on Seventh Street."

"He's still there?"

"Not him, his house."

"Should I bring my lock picks?"

"What? No! Why?"

"Aren't we breaking in?"

Murphy's face reddened. "No, we're not breaking in. Wait, why do you have lock picks?"

"I didn't say I had lock picks."

"Yes, you did."

"I simply asked if I should bring some. What are we doing then?"

"Looking, we're just looking. We're not going on a crime spree."

"Live a little."

Murphy realized it was time to retreat, so he did an about face and briskly strode toward his room. As he neared his door, he shouted, "Ventriculus!" Hogan scooted in behind him as he closed the door.

Chapter 11: Old Dead Lawyer

Murphy and Katrina pushed their bikes up Gold Street. It was a warm day with a light cloud cover. Gold Street was steep and it was easier to push rather than ride.

Murphy wore a black t-shirt and blue shorts and, as always when biking, his mat black climber's helmet. He was without his backpack and he felt strange. It normally went everywhere with him. But, seeing a large brown stain spreading at the bottom of the pack, his mom had discovered a half a bar of melted chocolate and had insisted it go into the washing machine immediately.

They stopped at the museum to return the letter to Mrs. Sutter, but she was out running an errand. Murphy left a note explaining everything and left it with the letter on her chair.

At the top of Gold Street, they mounted their bikes and turned left on Seventh. Katrina wore her mohawk helmet and mirrored shades. Murphy couldn't understand the choice of a pink fake fur vest for a bike trip, but he knew better than to bring it up.

Mr. Florence's house was the third on the right. As they approached, they saw a young woman on a ladder stretching from the front veranda to an upstairs window. She was tall and trim, her long blond hair tied in a single braid behind her back.

She was painting around the upstairs window. She reached high and dabbed paint with a tiny paint brush. A pint-sized bucket hung from the ladder. A deep forest green was covering up a faded pink that may have been red at one time.

Murphy noticed the ornate trim around the windows and the hand carved corbels under the gable. Both were things his dad had pointed out to him on occasion. He thought the house looked like many of the old homes in Juneau. His dad called them Juneau's Victorian treasures.

"Hello up there," Murphy called.

"Hello down there."

"Do you know anything about pirates or the *Black Skull*?" Murphy yelled.

"Sure," the blond woman said. "I know about Captain Hook and Long John Silver." She climbed down as she talked, careful not to spill her paint bucket.

Murphy and Katrina leaned their bikes against a low olive-green picket fence that separated the property from the sidewalk. They approached through an open gate and up a short stone walkway to the steps of a full veranda.

"Then, of course, there's Red Beard, Black Beard, and maybe even Purple Beard, I'm not sure. I can say I've never heard of *Black Skull,* only Beard."

She stepped off of the ladder and pulled off garden gloves covered with drops of green pant. "My name is Isabelle." She offered her hand.

"I'm Murphy." He shook hands with her and glanced toward Katrina. "And this is my, um, cousin Kat, Katrina."

Isabelle shook Katrina's hand. "Nice to meet you, um cousin Kat, Katrina. I love your helmet." Isabelle ran her hand through the bright orange mohawk.

Katrina ran her own hand through the mohawk before unbuckling and removing her helmet. "I like it, too." She smiled at Isabelle.

Murphy had noticed Isabelle's baggy t-shirt as soon as she stepped from the ladder. And he couldn't help but smile. It was bright yellow with a big brown poop emoji above the word "Happens." Like her gloves, her shirt was covered in drops of forest green paint. Drops and smears of creamy white and an azure blue also populated the shirt. She had a small smudge of green on her forehead.

"I mean real ones, Isabelle."

"Real what, Murphy?" Isabelle squatted down to place her paint bucket out of the way behind the ladder. Her knees poked through rips in faded blue jeans covered in red and yellow paint as well as forest green, creamy white and azure blue.

"Pirates, real pirates."

"I don't believe I know any real pirates. I've never met Black Beard or Red Beard, but that's probably because they died a few centuries ago."

Katrina spoke up. "Sorry, but he's obsessed with pirates. Hopefully you won't think he's crazy."

Murphy decided to change the subject. "Did you know Mr. Florence, the de—I mean, the lawyer who lived here?"

Isabelle rubbed at the small paint smear on her fore head with her index finger. "I know of him, but he passed away before I was born. I'm his great-granddaughter. He left this place to my grandmother and she gave it to me. My husband, Brian, and I are fixing it up."

"Have you ever heard of the *Black Skull*?" Murphy asked impatiently.

Katrina rolled her eyes.

Isabelle smiled. "No, I haven't. What is it?"

Murphy started to tell the story from the beginning, but Katrina nudged him and interrupted. "Murphy and I are trying to find out some info to help us prove a point. Well, he's trying to prove a point. I don't have anything better to do, so, you know, here I am." She gave a small curtsy.

Isabelle laughed and glanced at Murphy. "This sounds mysterious."

"It is kinda mysterious, Isabelle, we're trying to prove we saw pirates and a pirate ship called the *Black Skull* the other night in the channel."

Isabelle hesitated before saying, "Okay."

"Hey, hold up here." Katrina waved her hand as though she was trying to get her teacher's attention. "I saw a derelict old fishing boat and some shady dudes in rain gear." She pointed at Murphy. "Sherlock Holmes here saw pirates and a pirate ship called the *Black Skull*."

Murphy frowned at Katrina. "I know what I saw." He waited a beat before adding, "Watson."

He turned to Isabelle. "We found some info at the museum that mentioned your great grandfather. We were close by and wanted to see where he lived."

"He did," Katrina muttered quietly.

An expression of surprise showed on Isabelle's face.

"What's wrong?" Katrina asked.

Murphy felt a gust of wind pass between them. It ruffled his hair and his eyes followed a small dust devil forming in the gutter across the street.

Isabelle looked from Murphy to Katrina and back to Murphy before speaking. "A man came to the house recently. Brian and I were working on the interior then. He said his name was Mr. Fisher. He told us the same thing you just said, almost word for word. He said he found some info at the museum that led him to my great grandpa."

Murphy glanced at Katrina. "What did he want?"

"He said he was with the Juneau Historical Society and he was researching for a book he was writing. He asked if he could see any case files or other paperwork left from my great grandpa's law practice."

"Did you let him see them?" Murphy and Katrina exchanged glances.

"Oh, no," Isabelle said. "Like I told Mr. Fisher, there aren't any records or files."

"What happened to them?" Katrina asked.

"My grandma said they were lost when his office was flooded, way before I was born. We did show Mr. Fisher a couple of journals my husband found in a box in the eaves of the attic." Isabelle wet her finger on her tongue and rubbed at the green paint on her forehead. "He offered to buy one of them. We didn't sell it to him but I did copy some pages he was interested in."

"Could we look at it?" Murphy asked. "Please."

"I don't see why not. I'll go get it." Isabelle rose and disappeared into the darkened interior of the house. Before the door closed, Murphy heard a few notes from the Beatles' "Yellow Submarine." One of his dad's favorite songs.

Murphy and Katrina took a seat on Isabelle's front steps. A glint of light caught Murphy's eye. The sun was reflecting off a man's sunglasses. Murphy watched as the tall man turned into the covered entry of a house down the block.

The front door opened. "Sorry I took so long. I couldn't find my pitcher. The place is such a mess with all the renos we're doing. I can never find anything." Isabelle was holding a silver tray with a pitcher of lemonade and two glasses. She set the tray down and pulled two worn leather journals from under her arm. She handed one to Murphy and the other to Katrina. A slightly reddening spot had replaced the forest green smudge on her forehead.

"From just a quick look I think these are my great grandpa's personal diaries. I'm excited to read them and learn about my family history." Isabelle eyes wandered over the front of the house. "But I've been too busy with this." She gestured with both hands. "But this winter I intend to pour over them.

Anyway, you guys make yourselves comfortable, take your time and enjoy the lemonade."

She retrieved her paint bucket and brush. "I'm getting back to my job before it rains," nodding to a far-off cluster of ominous black clouds. "I'll be right up there. If you find any clues, you better tell me."

"We will." They said in unison. "Thanks, Isabelle."

"You're welcome, Murphy and Kat-Katrina."

Murphy squirmed on the wide step barely able to contain his excitement. He reverently opened the small journal, holding it carefully as if he feared it might suddenly explode in his hands, turn into dust, and sail away on a gust of wind, taking its secrets with it.

Chapter 12: Skeleton in the Closet

Murphy and Katrina were quiet as they read the diaries, turning pages while sipping drinks.

Katrina snapped her book closed. "This one ends before the court case." She passed the book to Murphy, took another sip and wiped away a thin lemonade mustache with the back of her hand.

Murphy was lost in reading. He absently put his hand out, took the book and set it beside his leg.

"Did you find something?" she asked.

He was silent. She waited a few seconds. "Yo! Earth to Murph."

He remained transfixed on the journal gripped tightly in his hand. His knuckles were white.

Katrina punched his arm.

"Hey!" he yelled.

"It's alive." She quoted from her favorite movie, *Young Frankenstein.*

Murphy heard Isabelle stifle a laugh from on top of her ladder. "You were right, Isabelle. These are your great-grandpa's private diaries."

He raised the book in his hand. "This one covers the time of the Blackwell case. Your great grandpa wrote about conversations he had with Blackwell, with the client-lawyer privilege thingy. Blackwell knew Mr. Florence couldn't repeat anything he heard. Because of that he felt free to tell everything. Your grandpa wrote that Blackwell refused any defense but wanted someone to hear his side."

Murphy took a long drink from his glass. An ice cube slid down and clinked on his front teeth. Katrina shivered.

"Blackwell, you said Blackwell?" Isabelle asked from her perch.

"Yes." Murphy replied. "He's a bad guy we learned about in a letter we found in storage at the City Museum." He finished his drink and placed the glass on the tray.

"When I made those copies for Mr. Fisher, I noticed the name Blackwell. It looks like you guys are following the same clues." She dabbed at a piece of gingerbread fascia with her brush.

Murphy stabbed a finger at the open page. He squirmed incessantly, something he couldn't help doing when he was excited. "Blackwell told Mr. Florence he buried the gold on the bank of a small stream that runs into Gastineau Channel."

"Which one?" Katrina asked abruptly.

Murphy flipped pages forward, then back. His eyes flitted across the words. "Doesn't say." He slowly lowered the book and stared into the distance.

"Nothing, there's nothing about where he buried the gold?" Katrina took the book from Murphy's hand.

He was deep in thought, his eyes not focusing on anything in particular. He felt the warm humid breeze on his face and heard the distant sound of cascading water from Gold Creek far below. He smelled cigarette smoke.

"Buried gold?" Isabelle called. "You didn't say there was buried gold. Of course, there is. Can't have a pirate story without buried treasure." She laughed. "We might have to sign a blood oath to divide the booty evenly."

"What about this?" Katrina nearly yelled. "This is un-freaking believable! You're sure no Sherlock ... you missed the best part."

She leaned toward Murphy. She was pointing at a particular passage in the journal. "This is fire. Read it."

Murphy sat up straight and grabbed the journal and began reading in silence, flipping a page every so often.

Katrina stared intently at the side of Murphy's face. Suddenly his body jerked and he nearly dropped the book. Katrina was smiling. "I know, hey."

"Holy cr...ow." He swallowed, opening and closing his mouth and swallowing again.

"What's going on down there?"

Katrina looked at Murphy. He was trying to talk but no words came out. His cheeks drained of color and he was perspiring.

"He's related to a murderer, that's all." Katrina announced.

"What? Does it say that in my great grandpa's diary?" Isabelle climbed down the ladder.

Murphy took a deep breath. "Th-that, Blackwell guy told your great grandpa that Blackwell was an alias he'd been using since he abandoned his family in California to come to the gold fields. I can't believe this." He lowered the book and sniffed the air. "His real name is Delgado." He spoke barely loud enough to be heard.

"Ta da!" Katrina shouted.

"I told you, it's the best part." She punched his arm. "This just made you way more interesting."

Isabelle stood above them. "Is your last name Delgado, Murphy?"

"It sure is." Katrina said.

"No way!" Isabelle exclaimed. She covered her mouth with her hand.

"Way!" They responded in unison.

Isabelle looked shocked. Her eyes were enormous and her hand fluttered in front of her mouth.

Murphy muttered in a monotone. "I'm related to a murderer?" He was counting silently with his fingers. "He was my great grandpa? My dad never knew his grandpa. He never said why. I guess we know now."

Katrina squeezed his arm. "Take a breath, Murph."

Isabelle lowered her hand and drew a deep breath of her own "This g-gets stranger by the minute." Her voiced faltered a little as she spoke.

There was a distant rumble far up the channel and they all turned in that direction. A brooding wall of dark thunder clouds stretched across the horizon and was advancing toward them.

Isabelle sat down between them on the top step. "Now I've got to tell you a story."

She crossed her long legs in front of her. "So, I've been restoring my great grandpa's desk in my spare time. Like I have any. Anyway, I found a key taped in the back of a drawer."

Katrina flipped pink tresses away from her eyes and turned to look at Isabelle. "Mysterious."

"That's what I thought, too." Isabelle smiled.

"I worked at a bank before we moved and I recognized the key was for a safety deposit box."

Murphy noticed a flash of light in Isabelle's eyes. It was followed closely by a clap of thunder.

"I was curious, so I took it to a few of the banks in town. On the third one, the Miners Bank of Juneau, the oldest bank in town, I got lucky. It was one of their keys. Of course, they wouldn't just open the box for me on my word. There were a couple days wait while they confirmed I was who I said and that it was my great grandpa's box."

A sudden gust of wind created a swirl of dust and dead leaves. They all watched as it raced up the walkway. They covered their faces and clamped their eyes shut as the debris sailed between them.

Murphy smelled cigarette smoke. It quickly dissipated and Isabelle blinked her eyes. Katrina coughed. Murphy plucked a dead leaf from the collar of his shirt, crumpled it up and tossed it in the air.

"It turned out my great grandpa Florence paid for that box into perpetuity. It hadn't been opened in almost forty years. But the rent was paid so the bank didn't care."

"What was in it?" Murphy asked.

Isabelle smiled at him. "That's the good part. Only a single sealed envelope was in the box."

Murphy looked disappointed but he asked, "Who was it addressed to? What did it say?"

Isabelle shook her head. "I don't know what it said, it wasn't for me."

"Who was it for?"

She smiled. "It's for you"

Murphy stared at Isabelle. "Why?" was all he could say.

Isabelle placed her hand on his shoulder. "I think I'd better explain. I didn't open the envelope because written on the front was 'For the Delgado family.' I was going to research the name when I had time this fall and try to get it to the rightful owners, but here you are on my front step." She laughed a little.

"You guys are the only Delgados I've ever heard of around here. Well, anywhere actually." Katrina spoke.

Murphy finally found his voice. "Yeah, me, too. I mean about the only Delgados. I've never met any others. I'll ask my dad."

"I'll ask the Internet." Katrina pulled her phone from her back pocket and her thumbs flew over the keyboard. "You are it. You and your parents are the only Delgados here."

"I think that takes care of that." Isabelle stood.

"I'll be right back with your letter, Murphy."

"Nothing to see here." Katrina smiled. "Only getting letters from dead murderers. Who knew hanging out with you would be so macabre?"

Murphy glanced at her. "Macabre?"

"Yeah, it means —"

"I know what it means."

"Well, it's my favorite word. And if I can't use it now, then when? Everything about this is macabre and I'm loving it."

"You would."

"Come on you have to admit getting a letter from a dead murderer is pretty cool, Captain Murphy Beard."

Murphy smiled. He didn't seem to mind her calling him Captain Murphy Beard. "Yeah, that is pretty cool, huh? It's also—"

"Macabre?"

"I was going to say freaky."

Isabelle stepped through the open doorway and handed Murphy an envelope. He heard the faint sound of classical piano coming from somewhere deep within the home.

"Here you go, Mr. Delgado. This must be a little strange receiving mail from the past?"

"Yes, very strange."

"Maybe you should open that with your parents. I don't want to be rude, guys, but I better get my project cleaned up before that gets here." She pointed toward the approaching storm. "It was so nice meeting you both and solving at least one mystery. You two have to promise to come back one day when you solve the mystery of the *Black Skull*."

"We will and thanks for the letter and the lemonade and it was very nice to meet you, too, Isabelle." Murphy stood and shook her hand.

"Thanks for the lemonade, it was nice to meet you, Isabelle." Katrina stood.

"You're welcome, Kat—Katrina, the cousin. I love your vest by the way." Isabelle smiled and turned to face her ladder.

"Thank you. I got it at the Thrift and Pick."

"Hey, Isabelle, what did he look like?" Murphy asked.

"Who? What did who look like? Or is it whom, I always mess this up. Anyway, who-whom are you referring too?"

"Mr. Fisher. What did Mr. Fisher look like?'

"Oh, him. Um, he was tall and thin and middle aged."

Murphy and Katrina exchanged glances as they strapped on their helmets. Over Katrina's shoulder, Murphy noticed a small puff of smoke coming from a doorway down the street.

Chapter 13: Pickpocket

They mounted their bikes and slowly pedaled toward Gold Street. They were deep in conversation, speculating on the contents of the letter as they passed a doorway to a squat stucco building a couple feet off the sidewalk.

Suddenly, a man stepped from the recesses of the doorway directly into Murphy's path. They collided and fell to the sidewalk in a tangle of arms, legs, and Murphy's bicycle. The man quickly jumped to his feet. He reached down with one hand to grab Murphy's bike and pulled Murphy to his feet with the other.

"I'm so sorry, young man," he said. "I'm such a klutz. I'm never watching where I'm going. Are you okay?" The tall man proceeded to dust Murphy off. He even turned him around and dusted off his back.

The man was wearing aviator sun glasses even though the sky was now quite dark. Katrina had put hers in her purse before they left Isabelle's.

"I'm fine, no problem." Murphy rubbed his elbow and stepped back from the man.

Katrina pushed her bike behind Murphy's and stared up at the tall man.

"I'm so sorry. Are you sure you are okay?" He stepped toward Murphy.

Murphy stepped back. "I'm fine, sir."

"Okay, you two have a great day then." He turned and walked away, saying sorry one more time over his shoulder as he turned the corner and disappeared down Gold Street.

Murphy stood in the middle of the sidewalk a little dazed and confused by the whirlwind of action. He ran his hands over his pockets. He pulled out his wallet and opened it. When he was satisfied the contents were intact, he put it away.

"That was weird," he said. "It felt like he was searching me for something when he dusted me off."

"Do you think he was a pickpocket?"

"I don't know if we have pickpockets in Juneau. I always thought they were something from Oliver Twist or only existed in New York City maybe."

"Look." Katrina pointed to the doorway where the tall man had come from. "That door's barred. He didn't come out of there. He must have been waiting for us to walk by. Look." She pointed to a small pile of cigarette butts just inside the doorway.

"You would think a pickpocket would try to steal a person's wallet, not check his pockets."

"Should we go to the police?"

"To be honest, I couldn't even describe him, aside from tall and thin and he was stinky like an ashtray. It all happened so fast. And I guess we can't prove he was trying to steal anything. Let's head home."

"Do you think he was trying to steal the envelope?"

Murphy didn't answer for a few seconds. "I don't know. I guess he could have seen Isabelle hand it to me."

"But he didn't see you hand it to me." She smiled and patted her purse.

"Maybe it was a good thing Mom hijacked my backpack."

"Yeah about that. Yuck, you're disgusting by the way."

"Hey, I didn't notice."

"You wouldn't. Boys!"

Murphy swung his leg over his seat. "I think I know what's going on and what's in the envelope." He cinched his helmet strap tighter. "I need to talk to Mom and I have to call Mrs. Sutter before we open it. Let's head back to Douglas."

They pedaled toward the corner of Gold and Seventh.

After a quick stop at the Breeze Inn convenience store, they pedaled south in the bike lane toward Murphy's house. They turned left on G Street when the brooding sky opened up above them as if a giant bucket of water had been poured over their heads. Lightning crackled behind them and was immediately followed by a thunderous boom. They were completely drenched in seconds.

They pedaled faster. They were only blocks from First Street and Murphy's house. He made a right on Second Street. He thought he heard laughter above the din of the storm and he glanced back. Katrina was also pedaling as fast as she could. Her pink high-tops were a blur. He saw her face was turned to the sky, she had put her mirrored sunglasses back on and she was laughing at the top of her lungs.

He shook his head, squinted his eyes, hunched lower over the handlebars and made a sharp left, turning down a dirt foot path that dropped off the sidewalk on Second. He raced down the hill, left the path that separated two properties and shot across the edge of Mr. Wallace's gravel driveway.

They both skidded to a stop beside Murphy's house, leaned their bikes against the wall and ran toward the front door. Murphy unstrapped his helmet and kicked off his shoes, leaving both where they landed on the floor of their entry hallway. Katrina hung her helmet on a hook and set her sodden sneakers neatly on the shoe rack.

"Murphy!" He heard his mom call from the kitchen. "Hang up your helmet and put your shoes where they belong."

Katrina smiled at him as she walked past. She left wet foot prints on the laminated tile floor.

As he was hanging up his helmet, he heard his mom say to Katrina. "Wow you are soaked, you better go change. I'll make tea."

Raising her voice, his mom called, "Murphy, go change. Make sure your wet clothes get into the hamper."

Chapter 14: Murphy's Theory

A half hour later, they sat at the breakfast bar. A steaming pot of tea sat on a pot holder surrounded by three cups, a small plate with lemon slices, and a jar of honey.

Murphy and Katrina sat across from his mom. Hogan was curled up under Murphy's stool. Katrina had changed into a light blue unicorn onesie covered in small rainbow-colored unicorns with the hood up. The pink horn stuck straight out in front of her.

Murphy's hair was a mess. After briefly toweling off, he hadn't combed it. He stirred a spoon full of honey into his tea. He was trying to get used to liking tea. It was his mom's favorite and Katrina had recently expressed an affinity for it. He was sure he would never get hot chocolate again but with enough honey, tea was tolerable.

"Mom, have there been any new holes?"

"You mean the ones we read about in the paper?"

"Yes, like the ones in Mrs. Jones' yard."

"Now that you mention it, today's paper had another story about holes. They found some on the Jefferson's property, next to Bear Creek."

"What are you guys talking about?" Katrina asked. She flipped her hood back. Her pinkish-purple hair was pulled into a pony tail and tied with a bright yellow scrunchie. He saw she was wearing tiny silver skull and crossbones ear studs.

He smiled. "Mom, did you ever meet the curator of the City Museum? He wasn't there very long before he quit. Mrs. Sutter doesn't like him."

"No, I wasn't aware they had hired anyone since Mrs. Smith passed away."

Murphy asked if he could borrow his mom's phone. "Just think, Mom, if I had my own phone, I wouldn't have to bug you all the time."

"I know, I know, son. Maybe the birthday fairy will be nice to you next month." She passed her phone to him.

"Ha, birthday fairy." Katrina snorted. "You should use the rotary dial phone in your dad's office."

Murphy stepped into the living room as he searched in the contacts for Mrs. Sutter's number at the museum.

* * *

Sonia and Katrina were sipping tea and chatting when he reentered the kitchen. He heard his mom say, "That's a story better told by Mr. Delgado. I'm afraid you will have to ask him."

Murphy set the phone in front of his mom.

"You're being secretive." She smiled at him.

"I needed to call Mrs. Sutter."

"Diane? She's one of my most favorite people. She teaches our Judo classes when Sensi Malcom is out of town."

Katrina spoke. "That's cool, she's awesome."

"You should come some time, Katrina."

"Hmm, maybe I will."

Murphy frowned.

She's already beating boys in wrestling. All we need is for her to learn Judo.

"I wanted to know what Mr. Carlson looks like." Murphy spoke up.

"Tall, geeky, and stinky." Katrina blurted.

"Why is that important?" his mom asked.

"Because that creep tried to pick pocket Murphy and he impersonated Mr. Fisher."

"What?" Sonia exclaimed loudly. "Who did what to you?"

Murphy explained everything that happened on their trip to return the letter to Mrs. Sutter and at Mr. Florence's house.

When he finished, his mom didn't speak. Murphy realized she needed time to process the news as was her habit before jumping to conclusions. He reached into the pouch on the front of his wrestling team hoodie and removed the letter with their family name written on it.

They were startled by a loud bang on the front door. They heard it open and slam against the shoe rack.

"Help!" His dad's voice boomed from the hallway.

Murphy, his mom, Katrina and Hogan rushed to the front door. His dad was sprawled half in half out of the open doorway, surrounded by plastic bags full of groceries. Oranges and tomatoes were rolling to a stop under the coat rack as Murphy rounded the corner.

John rolled over and rose to one knee. He hitched up his tan cargo shorts and stood. "Help me with these stupid groceries." His face was red and he was sweating.

"Forgot to bring the reusable bags that don't break, huh?" Murphy's mom asked her husband.

"No, I remembered to bring them."

"But you forgot them in the car again?"

"Okay, I forgot them in the car again." He stooped to pick up a loaf of French bread and a bottle of mustard.

They all worked quickly to retrieve the errant groceries and get them stored away where they belonged.

An hour later while his dad made his "Famous Spaghetti," Murphy got him caught up on the day's events. They were alone in the kitchen with Hogan who was watching for something to drop.

Murphy helped his dad tie apron strings behind his back. Emblazoned across the front in big block letters it said "Grill Dad" under crossed spatula and tongs. As he told his story, he watched his dad adeptly chop shallots, grate Parmesan cheese, and mince garlic.

"But why would Carlson knock you down and search you, son?"

"I'm sure he saw Isabelle pass me the envelope and I think he was watching her house because he knew about the letter and was figuring out a way to steal it."

"How could he know about it?"

"I guess people talked about Isabelle and the safety deposit box that her great grandpa had paid the rent on forever."

"I can see that. The small-town gossip line is alive and well." He pressed his hand down on a wide kitchen knife, smashing a clove of garlic.

Murphy saved the best part of his story for the last. He explained to his dad that Blackwell was actually a Delgado and was most likely his grandpa and Murphy's own great grandpa. He watched as his dad froze in place, a wooden spoon in one hand and a pepper shaker in the other.

John's face reddened, his brow furrowed and tears formed at the corners of his eyes. "I-I can't believe this." He slowly set the pepper shaker and spoon on the counter. He pulled out a stool and sat down heavily as though carrying a massive weight.

"All I ever knew about my grandpa," he looked at his son, "was that he abandoned your grandpa, my dad Bernard, and my grandma Elsa in California to come to Alaska to get rich mining gold."

Murphy heard the pan of water on the stove begin to boil. His dad didn't notice. Murphy took over and measured out four servings of spaghetti noodles using the hole in the wooden spoon as a gauge as he had seen his dad do many times. He added a pinch of salt and a splash of olive oil to the water. He gave the big pot of simmering red sauce a quick stir. He glanced both ways then dropped a chunk of Parmesan to the floor. Hogan scarfed it up like a high-speed vacuum cleaner, licked his lips, gazed up expectantly with his big brown eyes and waggled his stubby tail so hard his whole body moved.

"Are you okay, Dad?" Murphy put his arm over his dad's shoulders and gave him a squeeze.

John rubbed his eyes with his fingers. "Yes, I'm fine. It's a lot to absorb. I've spent a lifetime wondering about my grandfather and I know your grandpa Bernard was bothered by it until he passed away." He glanced at the stove. When he realized Murphy had done the spaghetti noodles, he smiled. He reached out and stirred the red sauce.

"I think he convinced Mom, your grandma Carol, to move to Alaska in hopes he might somehow find his father. The last time he saw his dad he was much younger than you. I'm glad he didn't find out his dad was a murderer."

John checked the noodles and again stirred the red sauce. He set the oven for 350° in preparation for the garlic bread and retrieved the French bread from the pantry.

"Can I see the journal? I just want to read it for myself."

"I'm sure Isabelle would be happy to show it to you. I pretty much told you all the good stuff, but if you want to check it out, she's really nice. Here's the letter she gave me. You should open it." He produced the aged envelope from his hoodie pocket and handed it to his dad.

John took it gingerly as though it might bite. "So, she found this in a safety deposit box at the Miners Bank of Juneau?"

"Yup and she found the key in the back of Mr. Florence's desk. Pretty cool, huh? Just like a mystery movie."

"It's fortunate Isabelle recognized it as a safety deposit key." John held up the letter to the florescent light over the bar. He turned it this way and that.

"Open it, Dad."

His dad was quiet for a long time as he turned the letter in the light. "Soon, son, soon."

Murphy smoothed his dad's "Famous Garlic Spread" on each half of the French bread, wrapped it in tin foil and placed it on the middle rack. He stirred the red sauce and turned off the element. He removed the boiling pot of noodles and dumped them into a strainer.

Better give Dad time to absorb this.

Chapter 15: The Map

After consuming the "Famous Spaghetti," they all enjoyed John's "Famous Tiramisu." They cleared the dishes and the four of them sat around the breakfast bar. Murphy's parents sipped espressos. Katrina had a towel wrapped around her head and was still wearing the Unicorn onesie as she scrolled on her phone.

Murphy heard Hogan in the hallway crunching down his dried dog food as he began wondering out loud what it all meant. "I think Carlson figured out that the *Black Skull* was a real pirate ship, or a real fake pirate ship. Just like we did. After he found the article about Blackwell and Mr. Florence and the hidden gold, he did the same thing we did. He went to Mr. Florence's house."

"Where he impersonated nice old Mr. Fisher," Katrina piped up. Her eyes never left her phone.

"Yes." Murphy replied. "He impersonated Mr. Fisher and pretended to be in the historical society. Good cover for his questions."

Sonia spoke up, "He might be a con man but he seems pretty smart."

John took a sip of his espresso and placed his cup on a saucer before he spoke. "So, after reading Florence's journal, and learning what Blackwell, or I guess, Delgado, said about burying the gold, you think that's why he suddenly quit the museum? To search for the gold?"

"That's exactly what I think, Dad. I bet he figured the idea of a pirate ship worked once to confuse people so he tried it again himself."

"But why?" Katrina asked. "Why would he need a pirate ship/creepy old fishing boat to search for gold?"

Murphy interlaced his fingers and stretched out his arms. Applying the right amount of pressure, he popped his knuckles.

"Stop that. I've told you a hundred times you'll get arthritis doing that. Do you want gorilla knuckles when you're older?" his mom chastised him.

"Gorilla Knuckles, great band name," Katrina retorted.

Murphy glanced at his dad who quickly looked away.

You're the one who showed me how.

Murphy hopped off of his stool, retrieved a glass from the cupboard and filled it with water from the pitcher in the fridge. He sat back down. "Kat, I think Carlson realized he couldn't just wander into people's yards and start digging. Mom said earlier there weren't homes and yards built along all the creeks back when Blackwell buried the gold. Carlson might be smart enough to figure if people have security cameras or motion sensors, they would be pointed at their driveways, not the channel."

"So Carlson is using the ship to sneak onto people's properties?" Sonia added.

"And if they are seen, no one will believe they saw a pirate ship just as the original gang thought," John mused.

"Tell me about it, Dad. They didn't build an actual ship but they made an old fishing vessel look like a pirate ship, black flag, sketchy name and all. Probably used the same name as a joke. They choose stormy nights and only go out late."

"So, they've been randomly searching yards in Douglas for buried gold?" Katrina asked.

"Not completely randomly," Murphy answered. "They know from Mr. Florence's journal the gold is buried next to a creek on the Douglas side of the channel. That eliminates Fish Creek, Gold Creek, Sheep Creek and any others on the Juneau side."

Murphy watched Katrina remove her towel and shake out her hair. She smoothed it straight back with her fingers and tucked stray pink strands behind her ears.

"Okay, so Carlson and his men pick a stormy night when no one is out. They anchor up by a particular creek, then sneak in and dig?" John asked.

"Yes, and if they are noticed, they have a quick getaway."

"And if anyone says they saw a pirate ship, who would believe them?" Sonia chimed in.

"He knows," Katrina giggled.

"Hey, you didn't believe it and you saw the ship and the men just like I did."

"I said I saw a sus old fishing boat. And guess what? It was a sus old fishing boat." She smirked and looked back at her phone.

"But made up to look like a pirate ship," Murphy responded.

"You're both right," Sonia intervened.

Hogan squiggled out from under Murphy's stool and disappeared into the front hallway. Murphy heard him lapping water from his bowl. He picked up the aged envelope and looked at his dad. "Dad, if it's cool?"

John nodded. "Go ahead."

Murphy held it up to the light, then looked at everyone in turn before he tore the end of the envelope open. He carefully removed two sheets of slightly yellowed paper. He gingerly unfolded the first page and spread it on the table. There was a short note in neat, precise cursive, written in faded pencil. Murphy turned the page toward his dad. "You read it."

John picked it up and held it carefully. He read it silently. Murphy noticed a small tremor in his dad's hand.

The page vibrated as John cleared his throat and swallowed hard. His Adams apple bobbed. He spoke hesitantly.

T—to Whom It May Concern.

If you are reading this letter, then two things are certain. One, I am no longer living and two, you are my relative.

I am sure you think of me as an evil man, and I will not argue. I do not ask forgiveness, and I do not make excuses. I chose the wrong path and I deserve to pay the consequences.

This map shows where I have buried the gold. Please do some good with it. Don't let it continue to destroy everyone it touches.

I first believed it should stay in the ground where it came from. But although I cannot make up for the past, now my hope is it can be used for good and somehow make a positive difference.

Sincerely, Frank Delgado

Be you discouraged not
When — causes fraught.
Like Davey Jones deep under
Stay the quest for thine plunder.

John pointed to the page. "This line is in the crease of the page and it's hard to make out the word before what appears to say burden. The word burden, like he carried a heavy burden."

Murphy leaned over the page and read where his dad was pointing. "I can't really make it out but it must say, my, like as in, my burden. That would make sense, wouldn't it?"

John read it again.

Be discouraged not.
When my burden causes fraught.
Like Davey Jones deep under.
Stay the quest for thine plunder.

"Okay, I guess that must be it." John lowered the page and placed it on the bar. Murphy noticed a far off look in his eyes; they weren't quite focused.

"What's up with the bad poetry?" Katrina questioned.

"Who knows, he was a murderer; he couldn't be all there in the head," Sonia replied.

Murphy spoke up. "I think it means, don't be discouraged if it's hard to find and we might have to dig deep." He unfolded the second sheet of paper and gently smoothed the crease with his hand. It appeared to be a crude map. Like the letter, it was drawn in faded pencil.

They all stared at a series of squiggly lines. No one spoke.

Sonia pointed at two parallel lines that ran horizontally across the page. "I think these two lines are the shores of the channel." She pointed where one line protruded to a rough point. "This looks like it could be the old tailing dump by Homestead Park."

Katrina put her phone in her back pocket. She pointed at a line on the page that intersected a horizontal line. "If that's the channel, this must be a creek running into the channel."

"They all are." Murphy gestured with his finger at nearly a dozen squiggly lines that intersected the meandering horizontal lines.

Katrina pointed toward the bottom of the page. "This must be the Juneau side, so we can ignore it."

"I count nine creeks on the Douglas side," Sonia commented. "From what I've been reading about hole sightings, Carlson and his gang have been working their way south. Digging at each creek."

"What's this?" Murphy pointed at a series of marks all clustered together along what they had already established was a creek.

Murphy squinted; it was hard to make out the faded marks. They looked like stacks of upside-down vee's clustered close together in rows.

"I think they're trees." John removed a pen from his shirt pocket and used it to point at what Murphy saw as upside-down vee's. "These are trees that are beside this creek." He used the pen to point at a line indicating a creek.

Katrina pointed as she counted. "Seven. When we saw the, er, pirates, they were on number seven if they are doing it in order starting at Nugget Creek here." She pointed at the first creek on the map. "We know they hit Iron Creek the other night when we saw them. They must be going to this one next." She pointed at the creek with the cluster of trees beside it.

"That's Anderson Creek," Murphy said. "It runs through Timmy's place, the Walkers. The whole family is in California on vacation."

"He's a jerk," Katrina muttered.

"But he's my friend."

"Surprise."

John was hunched over the map, studying it intently. "Murph, run and grab my magnifying glass from my office, please."

Murphy rushed off and returned quickly. He passed a large chromed magnifying glass to his dad.

John accepted it and held it over the cluster of trees on the map. He stared for a long moment. "Look below what we believe are trees. The largest one." He turned the page to Murphy.

Murphy took the glass. What he saw sent tingles through his body.

Is that an x below those trees?

Murphy nearly dropped the magnifying glass. When he looked up, he was grinning.

"What?" Sonia and Katrina asked at the same time.

Murphy almost shouted, "I think we found the gold!" He was grinning from ear to ear and squirming on his stool.

John was smiling, too.

Hogan rushed into the room, rose up, and put his paws in Murphy's lap. Water dripped from his mouth. Murphy hugged him and didn't care when he licked his face. Everyone was too excited to notice Hogan's transgression as they were all talking at once.

"Wait!" John's voice boomed over the clamor.

They all stopped talking and Murphy pushed Hogan off of his lap.

"If all of this is true, then Carlson and his gang could try Anderson Creek tomorrow night. The forecast is calling for the biggest storm of the summer. Sixty knot winds and heavy rain."

"Sounds like optimal weather for pirates." Sonia smiled.

"We have to call the police. The Walkers aren't home and it's perfect conditions for Carlson and his guys. There's no other way to stop them."

They quickly agreed that John would inform the police of the impending trespassing and property damage and possibly more about to happen at their neighbor's.

"Okay, I'll call them and let them know what's up." John walked toward his office at the back of the house.

"Off to use the serious phone," Sonia said.

Murphy laughed a little.

"His serious phone?" Katrina questioned.

"He really doesn't like modern things, and he acts like he can't figure out his cell phone half the time as an excuse to use his father's rotary dial phone."

Sonia spoke as she hopped down from her stool and placed her cup and saucer in the sink. "Believe it or not, we pay two dollars a month rent for that phone from the phone company. I'm thinking it's by now the most expensive phone in the world."

"And he wants me to have it, too." Murphy blurted. "I don't want it. It won't fit in my pocket."

"Ha, funny." Katrina laughed, but abruptly stopped and frowned.

Murphy knew she never wanted to let on when he made her laugh.

"Well, that was embarrassing." They were startled by John's voice behind them.

Murphy saw that his face was red and deep lines were set across his forehead.

"They hung up on me! They think I'm crazy. That cop told me to stop drinking or to start taking my medication." John gestured wildly with his hands. "He told me if I called again, he would trace the call, find me, arrest me, or take me to the psychiatric ward at Juneau General! What do I pay taxes for?" He plopped down on a stool.

Sonia stifled a laugh behind her hand. Murphy smiled and suddenly became busy under the bar petting Hogan. Katrina stared right at John's face. It was as if she was waiting for him to explode.

Sonia pulled herself together and in a mock serious voice, suggested her husband call the Coast Guard.

"You call them. I'm not calling anyone else." John slowly shook his head back and forth as he screwed up his face in disgust.

"Okay," Sonia agreed. "Maybe it's not such a great idea. We won't call anyone." She didn't try to hide her amusement this time and smiled at her husband. He smiled back and chuckled a little.

"I know, why don't we spy on them and collect evidence, then the police will have to believe you, Dad." Murphy spoke fast, squirming in his seat.

"No," his parents said in unison.

Sonia pushed her glasses up her nose with her index finger. Murphy noticed she was wearing the same color fingernail polish as Katrina's florescent lime green. Her eyes flitted back and forth between Murphy and his dad. They landed on Murphy and she stared directly into his eyes. "That's not happening. There's no way any of us are spying on criminals."

"It's not like they are violent ..." John began but was quickly cut off by Sonia.

"Not violent! Didn't that creepy Carlson assault our son today? And trespassing and vandalism are crimes and who knows what else they have done or will do. Gold makes people do crazy things. End of discussion."

"Okay-okay." John held up both palms in a blocking motion. "You're right, hon. They are violent and we are not messing with them."

"Everything has changed so much around here in the last hundred years. I'm guessing the gold has been plowed under or washed away or is deep below someone's foundation by now if any of this is even true."

"It's true, Mom. We proved it."

"I believe the Walkers' place, like ours, was a homestead site before Douglas was a mining town. Not much has changed on these properties. Mr. Wallace's place across the street as well."

Sonia scowled at her husband. "We need to get ready for the Old Timers' dinner at the Miners Hall tonight. You two can figure out how to catch pirates another day."

"Three," Katrina spoke.

"Hmm, you too?"

Katrina shrugged. "Hey, it's fun."

"And macabre?" Murphy interrupted.

Katrina looked at him as though he was bonkers. "Freaky, I was going to say freaky. Who says macabre?" She smiled demurely.

He frowned and got down from his stool. "But what about the gold?"

"Better yet, what about why Mrs. Sutter hates your dad so much?" Katrina piped up.

"She doesn't hate me exactly."

"She kind of does, sweety," Sonia ribbed him.

"Murphy said you destroyed her world. What does that mean?" Katrina asked.

"I don't want to talk about it." John shrugged and walked away.

Katrina looked at Sonia.

"Don't look at me." Sonia hopped off her stool and followed her husband out of the room.

"Murphy?" Katrina implored.

Murphy whispered as he walked past her. "I'll tell you later, I promise." Hogan hurried behind Murphy licking his hand.

Katrina was left alone in the kitchen. "What's wrong with this family?" she said to the empty room.

Chapter 16: Break In

Murphy stood in the small backyard of their home. There was a narrow strip of grass and a low picket fence between their house and the sidewalk that ran down their side of Front Street.

While he was waiting for Hogan to do his after-dinner business, his mind wandered as he watched an enormous, seven-decker cruise ship carefully approach its berth at the dock in front of South Franklin Street, downtown Juneau. Murphy was thinking about pirates, the *Black Skull*, Carlson and, of course, the buried gold.

Hogan inspected every blade of grass on the small lawn. He was consistent in his nightly search for the perfect place to go. It was a ritual that Murphy endured because he loved Hogan.

He was jolted out of his daydream when he heard a loud bang at the end of the street. It was followed by a low rumble that was increasing in volume. He watched as a beat-up, red pickup slowly passed by. Its windows were heavily tinted and he couldn't see inside.

Murphy didn't recognize it. The truck didn't belong to any of their neighbors. There wasn't much traffic on their street because it was a dead end and there were only four homes past theirs, two on each side of the street.

After the truck passed, he listened to it rumble across the tiny bridge over Iron Creek and approach the cul-de-sac at the end of the street. A high-pitched squeak pierced the night. He recognized it as the sound an older vehicle made when turning in a tight spot. Uncle Jerry's old van did the same thing. He said it was something to do with the steering.

The truck came back down the street. Murphy kept his eye on it as it crept by. He couldn't shake the feeling he was being studied by whoever was in that truck.

Hogan licked his hand. Murphy scanned the lawn looking for evidence that Hogan had finished and retrieved the pooper scooper from where it hung beside the trash cans.

After doing his part of the nightly ritual, he called Hogan and headed to the back door. As he opened it, he glanced down the street where the old truck had disappeared.

Just beyond Mr. Wallace's driveway and Mrs. Ivanov's house, past the old outboard shop and Mrs. Smith's upholstery store, there was a gravel parking lot where people parked their boat trailers when they were out on the water. Murphy could see the outline of a truck parked there now.

I've never seen a truck park in the boat trailer lot.

Murphy and Hogan entered the house and Murphy closed the door. He set up his game console in the living room before retrieving a glass of apple juice. He sat on the big L shaped couch that faced the front of the home and the big screen TV. He turned on the TV and sipped his juice. Hogan curled up beside him.

Hogan squirmed closer and caused Murphy to slosh a bit of juice on his favorite t-shirt with a green alien and a Sasquatch arm wrestling with the words: *Prove it didn't happen.*

He glanced at the window. It had grown quite dark outside. His eyes fell on the love seat across from the couch where a neat stack of blankets and pillows sat. Katrina was at a sleepover at one of her friend's homes. His parents were still at the Old Timers Dinner and would be for a couple more hours.

"Take that, you space goon," he yelled at the screen. "Ha-ha, extra power! Did you see that, Hoge? I got extra power again. I'll definitely get to level twenty this time, furthest ever."

Hogan raised his head, tilting it from side to side. A low rumble of a growl began deep in his throat. He looked around in every direction.

Murphy heard Fluffy barking next door.

"Geez, Hoge, I thought you would be happy, there's no reason to growl."

Hogan bolted upright, barked once and growled louder.

"It's just Fluffy. Calm down, Hoge." Hogan continued growling. "Maybe it's a black bear, huh, boy? Is it another black bear trying to get into our garbage?"

Murphy paused his game and set down the controller. "Let's go see what it is." Before he took a step, the room was plunged into darkness.

"Wow, the power's out."

Hogan lunged off the couch, jumping toward the sliding glass door in the front of the room.

"Settle down, boy." Murphy stepped toward Hogan, banging his shin on the coffee table. "Ouch, stupid table."

Moonlight occasionally peeked between the clouds, briefly lighting small areas of the living room floor. Murphy looked down, stepped around the coffee table and cautiously approached the sliding door and Hogan. He couldn't see much through the windows. Mostly his own reflection.

Hogan stood on his back legs, his front paws scratching frantically against the glass door. Murphy cupped his hands and peered out the window. A darkened face materialized inches from his own. Murphy screamed and stumbled backward. He tripped over the edge of the coffee table and landed on his back in the middle of the living room. The wind was knocked out of him, and for a few seconds, he lay motionless, desperately trying to draw air into his oxygen-depleted lungs. Hogan kept trying to claw through the glass door.

As soon as he could move, Murphy scrambled backward, crab walking across the living room floor. When he reached the hallway, he sprang to his feet and ran for his dad's office.

He slammed open the door and rushed to the old phone perched in the middle of his dad's desk. He picked up the handset and heard a dial tone. He pressed the receiver to his ear and spun the dial for 911. The dial tone disappeared. Silence boomed from the receiver.

"No!" He tapped wildly on the receiver. Nothing happened. He spun the dial but the phone remained lifeless.

He cut the phone line.

He could hear Hogan's continued assault on the sliding glass door.

No one is getting in that door. We need to go out the back way.

He slammed down the receiver and rushed to the front of the house and Hogan. He cupped his hands. The tall man was still there completely dressed in black with a black ski mask. He held an iron pry bar in one hand, raised over his head. He had what looked like a large piece of bloody meat in the other hand.

He's going to break the glass. Why does he have meat?

He turned and ran for the back door. "Come, Hogan!"

Murphy reached the door, sliding the last few feet on his socks. He released the locks and the chain, flung the door wide, and rushed outside. He took three strides, turned to see if Hogan was following, and slammed into something hard but soft. He heard a loud grunt. He bounced backward and landed on his rear on the wooden patio.

Someone clutched at his leg; he felt a hand grab the front of his shirt. A nasal voice spoke close to his ear. "I got yah, punk. Quit your squirming."

Murphy smelled mint and ashtrays as he struggled to free himself. "Let go of me! Let me go! Hogan, come!" He tried to focus on his assaulter.

Mickey Mouse? Why is Mickey—

Before he could finish the thought, a blur of fur and exposed teeth streaked past. The air exploded with snarls, growls and screams.

Murphy heard Fluffy in the distance barking his head off. He suddenly realized he was free. He rolled over to get out of the way and banged his head on the wooden bench beside the doorway. His vision went fuzzy, his tongue felt thick and it tingled. He touched his head and saw blood on his fingers. He lay still.

Over the din of snarls and grunts, he heard the nasal voice shrieking, "Get him off! Get him off me! Help me, boss. Help me!"

Murphy shook his head and rose on wobbly legs. "Hogan. Come, now." He reached for the door knob and glanced over his shoulder. A man rushed around the corner of the house. Headlights from a car turning on Second Street flickered across the figure. It was the tall man dressed in black. Murphy fumbled with the knob, then managed to open the door and rush inside. Hogan squeezed between Murphy's legs. He slammed the door, threw the deadbolt, and fastened the security chain. He slid to the floor breathing heavily. Hogan sat beside him facing the door, tilting his head back and forth and growling.

Murphy wiped tears from his eyes. He was scared but he was sure Hogan would protect him. He put his arm around Hogan and squeezed. Hogan briefly interrupted his growling to lick his ear. Murphy struggled to slow his breathing. He placed his ear against the door and heard a gruff voice. "What the heck happened to you?"

"I-I g-got attacked by a d-devil beast, that's what. It chewed my hand. Got my leg, too."

Murphy recognized the high-pitched nasal voice of the man who attacked him.

"Get up, Pew. You're not gonna die. I can't believe you got your butt kicked by a little boy and his puppy."

"Weren't no little boy, boss. He knocked me over. That weren't no puppy neither. That thing's a devil beast and it dang near gnawed off my hand."

"Get up, we need to get out of here. You've made enough noise to raise the dead," the gruff voice scolded.

"Sorry, boss. It hurts."

"I can't believe you brought a dang Mickey Mouse mask to a heist."

Murphy listened as the voices faded. He realized he had heard the gruff voice before.

Eventually, he rose and retrieved a baseball bat from his closet. He sat on the couch and waited for his parents. He hugged Hogan close as the dog licked his ear. Murphy noticed a spot of blood on his muzzle.

The pickpocket and the tall man dressed in black. They're the same guy.

Chapter 17: Aftermath

"Yes. Pew, like it stinks, pew." Murphy was talking to Detectives Ackerman and Ramirez in the back hallway of their home. Ackerman was a thin, red-faced man wearing a long tan overcoat and black galoshes that weren't fastened in the front. Murphy saw he wore dress shoes on inside the boots.

The detective's black hair was flecked with white. He had red bags under his eyes and an air of impatience about him.

Murphy sat on the hall bench while his parents stood behind with their arms around each other. His mom rested one hand on Murphy's shoulder. John had reset the main breaker; the lights were back on.

Detective Ramirez stooped, lacing his military-style boots. He was a fit, younger man with a trim blond mustache and a full head of close-cropped curls. He was dressed in jeans and a loose-fitting suede jacket. He stood up and smiled at Murphy.

Murphy had a small bandage on his forehead. The neckline of his alien vs Sasquatch t-shirt was stretched and his knees were dirty. Hogan sat beside him, pressed against his leg with his head in his lap as Murphy absently scratched his ears. The detectives were leaving after concluding their interviews and thoroughly inspecting the crime scene.

"Okay, just double checking. That's a pretty strange name and, if it's real, it should be easy to find in the data base." Detective Ramirez responded.

"I heard the other guy say it to the nasal Mickey Mouse guy, the one Hogan bit."

"And you're sure the guy in black was the same man that knocked you over on the street the other day?" Detective Ackerman asked.

"Yes, sir. He was tall and he had the same voice. I couldn't smell him though."

"You couldn't smell him?"

"Yes. I mean, I only heard his voice but, if it's the same guy that ran into me, he stinks like cigarettes."

"You did great, Murphy, thank you. Don't worry. We will find them."

Detective Ackerman made a hasty note in a small worn notebook, then tucked it into an inside coat pocket. He made a show of clicking his pen and putting it in his shirt pocket.

"We'll canvas your neighbors and see if anyone saw anything, especially an old beat-up red truck. Possibly a Ford, correct?" Ramirez asked.

"Yes, sir, I'm not totally positive but it looked a lot like the old one Brett Dirk drives on *Explore Rugged Alaska.* Have you seen it? The show, I mean."

"I think I know which show you are talking about, Murphy. My wife watches it." Detective Ramirez reached toward Hogan and patted his head. His loose jacket rode up exposing his gun and handcuffs. Murphy gawked.

"We will test the mask and the meat we found but I'm pretty sure this is a cow or moose liver." Ackerman held up a large plastic bag.

Ramirez reached out to shake Murphy's hand.

Ackerman reached past his partner and extended his hand to Murphy. "Thanks, son."

"Make sure you talk to Mrs. Ivanov, next door. Fluffy was going crazy. Maybe he woke her up and she saw something."

"Fluffy?" Both detectives asked in unison.

"Her dog, Fluffy, he's a British Bulldog."

The men stared at him but remained silent. Ramirez nodded at Murphy's mom. "We'll have a car come by every hour until nine tomorrow morning."

"You don't think—"

"No, ma'am," he quickly interrupted her. "We don't think they'll come back. Hogan and Murphy took care of that. It's only a precaution."

"Okay, thank you, detective."

When the door closed, his dad hugged him. "Are you okay, son?"

"I'm fine now, Dad, but I was really scared when it happened. If it wasn't for Hogan ..." his voice trailed away. Hogan's rear began to gyrate at the mention of his name.

"How's your head?" Sonia asked.

"It's nothing, Mom. I did worse when I fell off of the slack line at Twin Lake Park the other day."

"What?"

"Um, never mind."

"I can't let you out of my sight." She bumped him with her hip and tickled him under his arm. He squirmed out of her grasp.

She looked down at Hogan who stood looking up at them. "I'm sure thankful for this goofy dog." She reached down and scratched Hogan behind the ears. He spun his head and licked her hand before she could pull it back.

John hugged Murphy, patted Hogan's head and turned toward the bedrooms. "I'm going to get ready for bed." He disappeared around the corner.

"I'm pretty sure they were after the envelope Isabelle gave me, Mom. Carlson must think it has information about the buried gold. And he would be right. Until they know for sure, they will probably continue their pattern of digging. That means with the storm coming they could be digging on the Walkers' property tomorr— "

"Forget it, Murphy, you're not going. End of discussion."

"But, Mom."

"No buts. You told the detectives your theory. Let them investigate. They're the professionals."

She yawned and stretched. "It's so late. I'm mentally and physically drained. I'm going to bed and so are you."

John called from the hall bathroom. "Bed, Murph. Teeth, face and PJs. Let's go."

"Let's go to bed, Sherlock. Let the pros solve it," Sonia said.

"Okay, Mom."

But will they?

Chapter 18: Challenge

The afternoon the day after the bungled burglary, Murphy and Katrina sat on the couch playing Space Goons vs the Crock Men.

"You missed all the fun last night."

"Most def. It's usually so not exciting around here. Your mom told me about it when she picked me up at Delilah's. What did the police say about the map?"

"Not a lot. I don't think they believed me about that or anything really. How's Delilah?"

"Still oblivious to your existence."

"Mean."

"But true." She smiled.

"Whatever."

Hogan was balled up on the floor between their feet. His front paws were moving and he was whimpering quietly. Murphy waved his arms in the air, his fingers white where he gripped the game controller. His thumbs flew across the buttons in a blur.

"That doesn't help move your guy," Katrina said.

Murphy dropped his arms to his lap. "It can't hurt."

"So, what? They thought the map was a fake?"

He glanced out the picture window where white caps covered the channel. "I don't think they even thought it was a map. Detective Ackerman said it looked like a child's drawing of a centipede."

"And you told them about us seeing the *Black Skull*. What about Gretta's letter, did you tell them about that?"

"Yes, I told them everything. Florence's journal, Blackwell being my great grandpa, everything."

Katrina smiled and offered her fist. "You're the only one I know with a murderer for a great grandpa. Awesome and macabre."

He returned her fist bump halfheartedly. "Okay, but I'm not sure how great that is. Anyway, all the detectives talked about was another failed break in, up on Fifth Street last weekend. They found a broken basement window and blood, but no one got in. They are positive they are connected." His arms flew up and he twisted them this way and that, both of his thumbs flashed across the buttons. He dropped his arms back to his lap. "Fudge nuggets!"

"Ha! Space Goon down—Space Goon down. Crock Girl kicks butt." Katrina yelled, grinning. She reached out and punched Murphy's arm. "Told you I'd win."

"And so graciously," he groused. "Anyway, the cops think there are some amateur burglars roaming around. After they found the liver and Mickey Mouse mask, that's all they talked about."

"Look." Katrina pointed at Hogan. "He's chasing rabbits in his dreams."

Hogan's feet jerked. His tongue hung from the side of his mouth as he whimpered quietly.

"But they're going to stake out the Walkers' place tonight, right?"

Murphy heard a muffled thunder clap in the distance as rain began to hit the window. "I don't think so, Kat. They might patrol the neighborhood more, but I doubt they are staking anything out."

"What about your dad? Is he going to do anything?"

"No, he has faith in the police and Mom thinks the gold is already gone and she threatened to skin Dad and me alive if we go anywhere near the Walkers. Besides he flew to Kodiak a couple hours ago. He's overseeing an estate sale or something."

"Guess we'll have to go." She set down her controller.

"My mom would kill us both. Are you crazy?"

"Maybe, but I'm not chicken."

"Your dad would kill you too if he ever found out."

"And how would that happen? He's five hundred miles out to sea. Snitches get stitches."

"Okay, Alcatraz, chill."

Katrina flapped her arms and made clucking sounds. "Come on, your dad's gone, your mom has judo tonight. What happens after she gets home from judo?"

"She takes a long hot bath and watches her favorite show, Arctic Women."

"Exactly. We can slip out, check out the bad guys, take a couple pics and sneak back in. If we show the Fuzz the pics of Carlson and his gang trespassing and vandalizing the Walkers' yard, then they have to go after them."

"The Fuzz? Who are you, Scar Face?"

She flipped strands of long pink hair from her face and laughed. "I like old movies, sue me."

Murphy stood. "I'm going to lay down for a while. I didn't get much sleep last night." He wandered toward his room, yawing. He heard Fluffy barking. Fluffy hated thunder.

Hogan pushed between his legs as he closed the door. He heard Katrina clucking in the living room.

"Cluck-cluck-cluck ..."

Murphy paused at the door and rolled his eyes.

Why don't I have normal friends?

Chapter 19: Surveillance

"Shh, be quiet," Katrina whispered in his ear as Murphy stepped on a clam shell.

They were hunkered down under the front deck of Murphy's house. Moments before, they'd snuck out the sliding glass door after making sure his mom was in her bath.

"I don't think she can hear us over the wind." Murphy was wearing a long navy-blue rain coat and black rubber boots. His backpack was fastened tightly.

He looked up at the dark and brooding sky.

The light's fading fast.

"When we get there, I think it's easiest if we wade up the creek until we get to the Walkers' property. It's shallow; I did it last year."

A gust of wind flipped his hood off his head. He pulled it back on and cinched the drawstring. "If we hurry, we can hide before Carlson and his gang get there. Hogan, come."

Hogan materialized out of the gloom, pushed into Murphy's legs and licked his hand.

"Fire. Let's do this thing." Katrina snapped the top button on her slicker and started walking.

Murphy hurried to catch up with Hogan at his side. He took in her outfit. She was dressed head to toe in black. Black rubber boots and a black rain slicker that reached her knees. Her pink locks were hidden under a black night watchman's cap. To top it off, she wore skin-tight black gloves.

"Have you done this kinda thing before?"

"What kinda thing?"

"Never mind."

Lock picks, black gloves, hmmm.

Hogan was eager to rush after imaginary foes but Murphy kept him close. The tide was low as they walked near the pounding surf. They crossed a dry creek bed before treading cautiously around a wide bed of mussels.

White foam formed at the edge of the surf. He watched as it was picked up by the wind and rolled across the sand, reminding him of escaping cotton candy. The beach was wide in front of his house but narrowed as they approached a steep ridge that protruded out of the hillside and ran almost to the water's edge. Murphy breathed in heavily through his nose.

I love the smell of the channel.

Murphy pointed to the high ridge. "See those big spruce trees on top?" The wind was building fast and he had to raise his voice to be heard.

Katrina looked where he was pointing. "I see them."

"The big tree in the middle is Willy's Tree; we can hide there."

"Why does a random tree have a name?" She sidestepped a washed-up log.

"You know Willy Spencer?"

"Yes, he's in my math class."

"Well, a couple years ago, we were climbing trees up there with Caleb and Taylor. Willy fell out of that tree and broke his collar bone."

"That explains a lot." She laughed.

"It's been called Willy's Tree ever since."

"Of course, it has. Boys!"

They rounded the end of the narrow ridge. Murphy looked at the steep clay cliff. It rose from the beach to the top of the ridge, eroding from the wind and water. Fine dirt and small lumps of clay continually fell to the beach, forming dusty mounds that washed away at high tide. The rain was turning it to mud and small rivulets ran down the cliff face.

"Dad says our property and the Walkers' meet right down the middle of this ridge."

"Who owns Willy's Tree?" She wiped spray from her face with black fingers.

"Hmm, I don't know. Never thought about it. I do know Willy's mom banned him from climbing trees for the rest of his life."

After they passed the sluffing cliff, they reached a meandering creek that poured out of a canopy of willows bent over so far they were almost touching in the middle. Anderson Creek was approximately two car lengths wide and fairly shallow at that point.

"Here we go." He stepped into the creek and turned upstream toward the wall of willows. Hogan stayed in the heel position by his side.

Katrina followed close behind. The water flowed up their boots and reached a little above their ankles. It wasn't very swift and the going was easy. When Murphy reached the willows, he turned around and looked out at the channel.

"I bet they'll anchor up right there." He pointed at the rolling water not far from the beach. "And they'll probably come ashore right there and tie their skiff off to that rock." He pointed at the craggy rock sticking out of the sand on the far bank of the creek where it flowed into the channel.

Katrina took a quick look, then gave him a gentle push. "We better get going then."

He turned, bent low and entered the leafy tunnel. Stooped over, he was able to stay under the willow branches and make his way upstream.

The creek narrowed and became deeper. The water nearly reached their boot tops. The landscape was abruptly illuminated. Murphy blinked; he saw spots wherever he looked. A few seconds later, the air shuddered with a thunderous explosion.

Katrina let out a yelp. "That was close."

"I'll say. We need to get out of the water."

He passed under the last of the overhanging willows and stood up straight. Before them was an opening in the forest. On the left, the high ridge rose straight out of the creek. On the right, a flat grassy bank was bordered by tall spruce trees and brush. Murphy knew that beyond the tall spruce and the brush was a thicket of alder trees and further on there was the boat launch ramp and trailer parking lot beside the Douglas Boat Harbor.

He felt Katrina nudge his back. "Now what?"

He waded to shore on the right side and stepped up on a narrow grassy bank, turning around to pull Katrina up. She ignored him and hopped up effortlessly to stand beside him.

The narrow strip of grass ran a couple hundred feet to a low wooden fence and beyond that was a terraced garden, five rows in all. The terraces gradually ascended the slope to a two-story house and a small garage.

"It looks weird." Katrina spoke.

"What does?"

"The Walkers' place. I've never seen it from this side, only the front."

"That's the back. This is the front," he pointed at the house.

"Oh, yeah. I guess it is."

Murphy turned away from the house and peered across the creek. "There's a trail to the top, around that curve in the cliff." He pointed to a short narrow gravel bank in front of the steep wall.

A gust of wind gained momentum as it approached from the channel. The willows overhanging the entrance of the creek began to quake, then roil as if being stirred by a giant spoon. Murphy noticed the creek surface was agitated and small white caps were forming. The roar of the wind was intense and increasing. They turned their backs and hunched over as the gust hurtled past. It was gone in seconds.

Murphy swiftly stepped back into the creek and began crossing, Hogan by his side. "We need to hide before the next one comes," he called over his shoulder.

"Right behind you."

They crossed the creek quickly and approached what at first looked like a sheer wall. Murphy made his way along the base of the cliff on the narrow gravel bar. He touched the wall as he went. He rounded a protrusion and disappeared. Katrina followed closely.

"There it is." He pointed upward at a narrow draw in the side of the cliff. A crude trail ascended straight up. It would have gone unseen by anyone who didn't know it was there. It was more a ladder than a trail. Stunted spruce trees desperately clung to the cracks in the rock and were bent and twisted at odd angles.

Another flash of lightning allowed them to see clearly for a split second. The trail rose roughly twenty feet, made a right turn and disappeared around the edge of the wall.

They both jumped at the next clap of thunder. "You'll have to grab roots and rocks to pull yourself up and be car—"

Katrina brushed past him and sprang upward. He watched as she climbed nimbly, quickly reached the turn and vanished. He looked down at Hogan. Hogan looked back and wiggled.

"Well, go get her then." Hogan bounded after Katrina.

"It's okay, I'm good here. You guys go ahead." Murphy began the climb. He grasped an exposed root and pulled himself up to stand in a small clearing on top of the ridge. Hogan lunged into him, stood on his back legs and licked his face.

"Down, boy, it's only been thirty seconds."

Murphy looked toward the cluster of enormous spruce trees that dominated a small clearing. Seven in all, each impressive in its girth and height but one in particular towered over the others. Katrina was sitting on the edge of the cliff. Her legs dangled as she kicked them back and forth. She overlooked the grassy bank of the creek where they had stood moments before.

The wind gusts steadily grew stronger and the spruce trees waved and groaned. Murphy gazed up at the largest of the trees and spied the thick branch that Willy Spencer had fallen from, landing on his head. He smiled at the memory.

Katrina called out. "I thought you must have forgotten something and gone home for it." She pretended to yawn.

Murphy tried not to smile. "Life is in the journey, not the destination."

"Way to steal quotes from Vista Cruise Line commercials."

"Whatever. Do you see anyone yet?

"No. And it's getting harder to see anything."

Murphy looked up at Willy's tree. "We better hide." He nodded toward the huge spruce. "See where those three branches all come out of the trunk at the same place?" He indicated where three thick branches created a nest-like area.

"We call it the fort. We were hanging out there the day Willy fell." He walked to the base of the tree. The first branch was the same height as the pull-up bar at Twin Lake Park. He turned to Katrina. "Do you want a boost?"

She approached the tree, leapt to the branch and swung her legs up and around and, in a second, she was on top of the branch. As she'd flipped upside down, water drained out of her rubber boot and splashed on Murphy's face.

"Hey!" He sputtered and wiped the water away.

Of course, she doesn't need help.

Murphy instructed Hogan to hide and be quiet. Hogan stared at him with his big buggy eyes. He reared up and put his forepaws on the big tree. He looked up, then looked at Murphy.

"Sorry, buddy, you can't climb trees." Hogan wiggled his rear. "Good try, Hoge, now go!"

Hogan walked slowly toward a snarl of brush that grew under the farthest spruce. He looked back often, but he did what he was told and eventually vanished in the dense brush.

"Stay until I call you."

A half hour passed as they were secure in their nest fort. They had a full view of the narrow grassy bank that ran beside Anderson Creek and could see the Walkers' house and garage. There was a dim light on at the back of the house.

Katrina lay curled in the bowl of the branches where they joined to the tree. Her black hat was pulled low and her hands were stuffed into her rain slicker pockets.

Murphy straddled a large branch a few feet above Katrina. He leaned against the mighty tree and strained to hear above the mounting storm. He twisted his body and looked down the beach the way they had come. "Looks like Mom's watching her show."

Katrina twisted to see. The lights of Murphy's home glimmered faintly in the mist. A blueish light glowed from the nearest window.

"Hey, that's your place."

"Yup. We may survive your crazy idea after all. I mean I would rather get caught by pirates than my mom."

"How's your arm?" she asked.

"My arm, what's that have to—"

"I don't remember twisting it behind your back."

"Okay-okay, our crazy idea." He rolled his eyes.

The tree swayed and a dead branch fell past them to the ground. As though they were at the center of an explosion, their world abruptly illuminated. The ground shook under another clap of thunder. Fat rain drops fell from the dark clouds.

"Is it a good idea to be in the tallest tree while lightning is striking?" Katrina's voice quivered.

"This tree's been here forever and lightning hasn't hit it yet."

"There's always a first time. This is way sketchy." She glanced nervously toward the sky. "Lightning freaks me out."

The rain increased in volume. The tree gave some protection from overhead but the wind blew the water straight at them.

"I'm going down. I'll stay low and watch from the edge of the cliff." She swung her legs over the nearest branch.

"Hey, where you going?"

"I'm not staying up here to get fried. I'm going down, I'll be fine." She swung off the thick branch to a lower one and then shimmied down the trunk to the ground.

"Turn off the flash," he called after her.

The darkness was near total, but he could see motion as her black form moved to the cliff edge and melted into the ground.

Murphy understood Katrina's real fear of the lightning, but it unnerved him to see her unnerved. She was normally unflappable. He strained to see where she lay as he listened to the worsening storm and kept his eyes on the creek and the grassy bank. Anderson Creek appeared as a black snake. Glimmers of light on the far bank's pale green grass gave him the feeling of looking down at the Milky Way. The single light over the Walkers' garage door flickered as it was pounded by the gale.

A strong gust blew off of Mount Roberts straight across the channel and ripped along the top of the ridge. The rain wasn't actually falling but was flung in every direction by the wind.

Murphy's eye caught something below. He stared at the spot. There it was again. A tiny prick of light from the direction of the overhanging willows. It became a twinkle, then was solid. He saw movement around the light. Silhouettes of men.

They're here. We were right.

Chapter 20: Carlson's Gang

The gang waded up the middle of Anderson Creek. Their light swung back and forth as they waded, dimly illuminating three men. One was much taller than the other two. The tall man carried the lamp. Another man had two shovels. The last man limped as he carried the metal detector. A white bandage on his hand reflected in the light.

Where is the fourth man?

The men made their way to the far bank. Their voices carried in the wind, but they were too far away for Murphy to make out their words. The man with the shovels pointed across the creek, but the tall man pointed to the ground under their feet.

Must be Carlson.

The wind buffeted the three men and their slick rain gear flapped in the wind. The tall man set the lamp on the ground and grabbed the metal detector. He hunched over it for a minute before running the round disk over the ground. He slowly walked along the grassy bank. Almost immediately, he stopped and swept the metal detector in circles. Murphy could hear the beeping from his hiding place.

Murphy was distracted when a small light appeared below him near the edge of the cliff. Katrina had her phone out.

Carlson waved the other men over and pointed to the ground. They immediately began digging. They broke through the layer of grass and sod and continued to dig.

Eventually they stopped. One man knelt and ran his hand around the bottom of the hole. He looked up and shook his head. Carlson ran the detector over the hole and it beeped again. The men dug deeper. This continued until they eventually found something. The bandaged man held it out. Carlson examined the object, held it near the lantern, shook his head, and tossed it into the creek. He began running the detector over new ground. Almost immediately, Murphy heard the beeping again.

The same scenario continued over and over. Carlson found something of interest with the metal detector and his partners dug it up. Murphy couldn't tell what they were finding, but judging from Carlson's reaction, the items were not of value.

Murphy remembered his mom telling him the ground around Douglas was saturated with nails, cans, railroad spikes, ball bearings, and other odd bits of metal from the mines and fires. He smiled remembering Uncle Jerry digging and swearing and throwing stuff away and swearing some more.

The gang dug from the lower end of the flat bank closest to the channel and moved toward the Walkers' property. The wind grew stronger and it became harder to hear their voices and the beeping.

Every so often, Murphy glanced down at Katrina but could only see the faint glow of her phone. He bit the inside of his cheek and tried desperately not to fidget.

The sharp and unmistakable crack of a stick breaking underfoot, loud even over the roar of the storm, froze him in place. It was close. Murphy managed to stifle a startled gasp. Every muscle in his body tensed.

Is it Hogan? He wouldn't break command, would he?

"What yah doing there?" a deep voice resonated in the dark.

"Stay where you are. Get those hands out where I can see them. Don't try anything funny, I'm pointing a gun at you."

Murphy couldn't see the man in the dark, but he noticed movement near where he'd last seen Katrina. The man's voice scared him and the mention of a gun sent chills up his spine.

A tiny beam of light illuminated Katrina's black form as she slowly stood up. The gunman held a pencil flashlight and she was frozen in its beam. Rain splattered her upturned face but she remained perfectly still.

Murphy watched helplessly. In the faint glow, he could make out the hulking man towering over her. He was dressed in a shiny rain jacket and pants. His hood was pulled up obscuring his face, but Murphy could see a long, bushy, black beard flapping from his chin. A glint of light reflected off a shiny surface in a gloved hand. Murphy inhaled sharply as he realized the enormous man did have a gun and was pointing it at Katrina.

Murphy heard the man's gruff voice. "Hey, you're a girl."

"Thanks, Captain Obvious. What gave it away?"

"With a smart mouth, too. Why are you filming my friends? Who is with you?" The large man glanced about but held the pistol on Katrina.

"I'm bird watching and I work alone."

The wind ebbed for a moment while another rampaging gust was building up out on the channel.

"Yeah, right," the man grunted. "Where are your friends, little girl?" He nervously surveyed the small clearing.

Murphy watched as the tiny light danced on Katrina's face. She stared unblinking, shrugged and responded, "I don't like friends, so whatever."

She faked a yawn. Murphy knew it was something she did when she was hiding her apprehension.

The big man shook the pistol at her. "I don't think so, girly, there's no way you're out here all alone on a night like this.

What are you, ten? Do you have parents or are you being raised by wolves?"

"Funny. Try twelve. Look who's talking, Kodiak."

The big man didn't reply.

"Were you raised by grizzlies?" she asked.

Murphy shifted his body slowly and silently, a fraction of an inch at a time until only the top of his head showed over the massive branch.

The man continued to search the area, keeping one eye on Katrina the whole time. He moved a few steps to the side and took a quick look behind Willy's Tree.

Please don't look up.

As if he heard Murphy's silent plea, the massive man glanced up. He swiped at a long lock of black hair. He shielded his eyes with his other hand. The rain hit his eyes and he blinked rapidly.

Murphy closed his eyes and attempted to melt into the tree branch.

"What gives, Sasquatch, do you think that I'm traveling with a troop of monkeys?" Katrina's voice carried over the wind. "The monkeys are busy, it's just me, but watch for falling coconuts."

Murphy heard a loud crack as the man stepped on another dead branch as he moved toward Katrina. "Let me see that phone."

With surprising speed, he grabbed her phone from her raised hand. "How do you open it? Let's see all your bird pics then."

"I'm not opening it and stop pointed that thing at me. What's wrong with you? Are you afraid of me? Does the giant ogre need a gun to handle a little girl like me? I bet you were a bully in school. Did they even have school way back when you were a cub or did momma bear den-school you?"

Murphy cringed as he listened to Katrina goad the man. The giant didn't say anything for a long time. Murphy was worried Katrina might have provoked him too far.

The man reached into his pants pocket, produced a small multi-bladed pocket knife, and thumbed open the largest blade. He brandished it in front of her face.

Murphy held his breath and watched the light from the small flashlight glint on the blade. He saw the distinct red handle with the white cross.

Katrina didn't blink.

The man spoke but the wind was gaining in power and Murphy missed the words.

Lightning flashed and, for a second, he could see everything clearly. He saw the broad back of the man, his jacket slick with water, his hood pulled up. He saw him pocket a silver revolver.

Murphy pulled his head back behind the massive branch. The light faded and the wind blasted the small clearing around the mighty trees. Murphy held on tightly.

As the gust passed, he heard the man say, "You're right. I don't need a gun, besides it might make too much noise if I have to shoot you. My trusty knife will work just fine so don't get any stupid ideas." He shone the penlight at the phone. "I'm sure my boss will get you to open this."

He stuffed Katrina's phone into another pocket. "Let's see what he has to say about you and your birdwatching story. Get moving. Don't try anything fast."

"Why do you need knives and guns? What could I do against a big scary man like you?" She smiled and batted her eyes lashes.

The huge man laughed. To Murphy, it sounded like a moose.

"Move it, girly."

Murphy watched as Katrina led the way toward the narrow draw and the only trail leading down. He heard her voice over the storm.

"Don't push, gorilla man. I'm going. Be careful with my phone."

Their voices faded into the dark. Murphy released his grip on the branch. He hadn't noticed how hard he'd been squeezing; his hands hurt.

What am I going to do? What will they do to her? I never should have agreed to this. Would he hurt her? At least one of them has a gun. Where's Hogan?

He realized Hogan hadn't made a sound the entire time the gunman was abducting Katrina.

Did that man hurt Hogan? Is he okay?

Murphy quietly descended the massive spruce tree. When he reached the ground, he whispered, "Hogan, Hoge? Are you okay? Come on, boy, where are you?"

A commotion sounded in the bushes by the edge of the tiny clearing. Hogan popped out and rushed to him. He jumped up, resting his paws on Murphy's shoulders attempting to lick his face. Hogan was dripping wet and his paws were muddy.

"Get down! Sit. Where have you been? Why were you hiding in the bushes like a scaredy cat?"

Hogan sat in front of Murphy and stared up intently. He cocked his head as if to say he was listening. "Stay."

Murphy crawled toward the cliff. Hogan lay down, put his nose in the dirt and watched Murphy from the top of his eyes.

Murphy inched his way to the brink of the cliff and cautiously peered over. The tiny flashlight beam bounced below, moving closer to the lantern and the three men standing in the shadows around it. In the dim glow of the tiny light, Murphy watched as the gunman and the smaller form in front moved to meet the other men.

Carlson waved one arm in the air and held the lantern in the other. He gestured toward the gunman and Katrina. Soon they were all animated. The man with the gun turned and pointed to the top of the cliff. Everyone followed his arm. Murphy froze, not daring to breathe, wishing he could make himself smaller. The men soon looked away and resumed their heated discussion.

The big man fished Katrina's phone out of his coat pocket and handed it to Carlson who fumbled with it until it lit up. He held it up to Katrina's face. At intervals, he looked from the tiny screen to Katrina and then back to the phone. Eventually, he shook the phone at her, threw it to the ground and stomped on it with the heel of his boot.

Katrina remained completely still.

Carlson looked around the clearing. He wiped water from his eyes and continued to survey the area. He ran his gaze across the top of the ridge. He said something to the man with the long beard who shook his head vigorously and shrugged his shoulders.

Carlson's lips were moving as he gestured to his men. It was obvious they were getting ready to leave. And they were taking Katrina with them.

Now what? What can I do?

He backed away from the edge. His mind whirled with troubled thoughts.

My friend has been kidnapped at gunpoint. What if Carlson gets back to the Black Skull and disappears with Kat? What have I done?

Chapter 21: Race to the *Black Skull*

Murphy realized that it was up to him to save Katrina. *There's only me and Hogan. Hogan?* He crawled to where Hogan lay and hugged him. "I'm sorry, boy. I know I told you to hide and stay. You did a great job. You're a good boy, Hoge. I love you and I'm sorry."

Hogan sat on his haunches and licked Murphy's face. Murphy let him for a moment before ordering him down.

He tore off his backpack and plopped it down between his knees. At first, his fingers fumbled with the zippers, but he quickly tore through the multi-pocketed pack. He extracted a small sheet of note paper and a fine-tipped black marking pen.

Resting the paper on his knee, he scribbled a note. As soon as it was written, he turned to Hogan who had remained sitting close beside him.

Murphy rolled the note into a slender tube, reached into the largest pocket of his backpack and retrieved a small half-sandwich bag. He tilted it up and shook out some bread crumbs. He placed the note in the bag and zipped it closed. Then he tied the note to Hogan's collar with a piece of string.

Murphy pulled the string tight and held Hogan's head in his hands, staring directly into his eyes. "Okay, Buddy. I know you want to stay but you have to do something more important. I need you to take this note to Mom. Go straight home. No sniffing all over the neighborhood or begging at Mrs. Turner's. Straight home, do you hear me? Kat needs us."

Hogan cocked his head and gave Murphy a quick lick on the face. "Thanks, Hogan. Now go! Go home, Hogan. Go to Mom, boy. Go to Mom."

Hogan looked confused, he glanced where Murphy pointed and back. Then he stood and trotted toward the trail. Before he disappeared into the darkness, he paused again and looked back.

Murphy pointed. Hogan turned and disappeared.

Murphy scrambled back to the cliff edge just in time to see the gang leaving. They were in a single line entering the shallow water of the creek. Carlson led the procession holding the lantern. Katrina was directly behind him followed by the large man with the gun.

Lightning cracked nearby and the clearing was illuminated. Murphy pulled his head back. The ground shook and his ears popped. When the light faded, he risked another peek over the edge.

Carlson was nearing the willow canopy. The man behind the gunman carried the shovels. He had no distinguishing characteristics other than he was the shortest and his face was covered. The last man limped and struggled to carry the metal detector.

Murphy wiped water from his eyes with his fingers.

I've got to help Kat. Can I get to the Black Skull before them? And what if I do, then what?

He snatched up his backpack and ran toward the beach, cinching the straps as he moved. He raced along the ridge, following a faint animal path he could barely see. The men far below couldn't hear him over the wind, so he traveled as fast as he could, ignoring the noise he made crashing through clumps of brush and careening off low-hanging limbs. His mind raced as fast as his legs pumped.

How am I going to get down? Can I beat them to the beach? How will I get on the Black Skull?

He scrambled over moss-covered boulders and fallen logs, not caring about scrapes and bruises. He skirted a jagged outcrop of rock before throwing himself at a wall of dead brush. Instead of meeting the fierce resistance he expected, the barricade of vegetation gave way easily and he reeled out of control. His momentum carried him over the edge of the clay bank. For a moment, he was weightless. Then he slammed down hard on his back.

His breath exploded from his chest. He desperately tried to fill his lungs as he started cartwheeling out of control. He spread his arms and legs in an attempt slow his chaotic decent. It was a trick he'd learned snowboarding at the Juneau ski hill. The tumbling stopped but he continued to slide headfirst on his back through a slick layer of mud. He managed to flip over onto his stomach, immediately slamming face first into a mound of mud.

Stunned, Murphy gulped for air. Tiny lights floated in front of his eyes. Tears trickled down his muddy cheeks.

Eventually, he drew in a breath of clean, cool sea air. He spat out mud and swiped at his face with dirty fingers in an attempt to clear his vision. His fingers left lines of clear skin in the mask of mud that covered his face.

He picked himself up and stood erect. Everything hurt. He touched his forehead and felt a lump. His pant leg was torn. He rubbed a sore elbow and glanced at his bleeding knee.

I'm okay. Now what?

Chapter 22: Stowaway

He looked in every direction. He was alone on the beach. He'd beaten the men. A few yards down the beach, he spied the small skiff he'd seen the first night. It was pulled up on the sand and tied to a rock.

Right where I had predicted.

Beyond the skiff and barely visible in the mist, the Black Skull rose and fell in the turbulent waves. It rode taut on its anchor chain swinging back and forth like an eager dog on a leash.

Murphy ignored the pain in his knee and his throbbing head. He was completely exposed on the beach as he crouched low and ran toward the skiff. He skidded to a stop beside it and laid down below the gunnel.

He peered around the bow toward the creek mouth. There was no sign of the gang, so he took a quick peek inside the skiff. He saw two oars floating in a couple inches of dirty water. He looked toward the *Black Skull*.

Even if I could swim to it, there's no way I can get over the rail, it's too high.

He snuck another look in the skiff and noticed a piece of plywood covered a short section of the bow, a poor attempt to make a dry storage area. The wind shifted slightly, carrying voices to him.

Murphy acted immediately. He scrambled a few feet to the creek, crawled in, washing off as much mud as he could. Then he belly-crawled back to the skiff and slithered over the side.

The voices were close as he scrambled under the plywood. He felt a life vest under his body. He shoved it ahead of him. His fingers found a torn scrap of canvas sail and he quickly pulled it over himself. He scrunched into a tight ball and rested his throbbing head on the life vest.

Carlson's voice rose above the wind. "Hurry up. We need to get out of here now before someone comes looking for little miss spy here."

Murphy stared at a smear of mud on the skiff's gunnel. Every so often a fat drop of rain hit it and washed a bit away.

The sound of rocks and mussel shells crunching under feet reached his ears. He recognized the voice of the man who'd captured Katrina.

Not fast enough. Will they see it?

"I'm not a spy." It was Katrina's voice.

"Shut up and get in the skiff." Carlson said.

The last bit of mud dislodged itself from the gunnel and slid down into water in the bottom of the skiff. The trail disappeared in seconds. Murphy took a silent deep breath.

The sky lit up, and the air reverberated with a tremendous burst. Thunder echoed off Mount Roberts and rumbled down Gastineau channel.

Murphy was thankful for the storm. The sound would cover any noises he made. He worried one of the men might want to use the tarp. Even if they pulled it away, he hoped they wouldn't see him in the shadows.

"Hurry up, Pew," Carlson yelled.

"I'm coming, boss." Murphy recognized the voice of the man who attacked him at his house.

The skiff slid backward and Murphy felt it rise and fall as the waves smacked it into the beach with jarring thuds.

"Push us off when we're all aboard," Carlson yelled above the crashing of the surf.

"On it, boss."

"Bones, get her loaded up and keep an eye on her. Stow those tools and help shove off."

"Yes, sir."

Murphy felt a sharp pain in his ankle. He stifled a yell. One of the thugs had tossed the metal detector into the bow, hitting him. He bit his lip and concentrated on making himself tiny. A shovel glanced off of his shin. He bit down harder on his lip, tasting blood. He wanted to rub away the pain but he didn't dare move.

The skiff rocked erratically. Murphy could feel the boat being shoved backward. Then it spun around and the bow began bucking the waves. The men grunted and the oarlocks squeaked with every pull. He risked a quick look, opening only one eye. He was surprised how close the man was to him. The behemoth's back obscured his view.

In a few minutes, the skiff bumped into something solid.

We must be at the Black Skull.

"Get the tools and the girl up the ladder," Carlson yelled. "Take her below and tie her up while I figure this out. Get this skiff tied off to the stern. Weigh anchor. Run up the main sail. Let's get this tub underway."

Murphy felt the boat get lighter as each man stepped off. All he could do was lie low and wait.

The ship's anchor chain clanked as it wound around the capstan. Unfurling sails flapped in the wind. Murphy cringed as the skiff slammed against the larger vessel. But then it stopped and the skiff bobbed lightly in the swell. Murphy slowly lifted back the tarp, cautiously crawled from his hiding place and peered forward over the plywood bow cover.

The skiff was tied to the stern of the *Black Skull* and was following obediently behind. The *Black Skull* was running without lights and was indistinguishable in the dark.

Great. Now what am I going to do?

The hard rain fell and the salty spray from the waves stung his eyes. He pulled the tarp close to stop his shivering while he took stock of the situation. The skiff was tied to the *Black Skull* by a thick, braided line, a rough manila rope almost as thick as his wrist. Just like the slack line at Twin Lakes Park, the park where he and his friends often played.

The best he could tell, the line between the two vessels was not as long as the slack line at the park. He'd been trying to pull himself across it, hand over hand without falling for months now. He had almost succeeded last time. But he'd never tried it in the pouring rain with salt spray stinging his eyes or in the dark while bobbing behind a pirate ship.

Maybe I can pull the skiff closer to the Black Skull.

He climbed to the point of the bow, grasped the line in both hands and pulled with every muscle in his body. Nothing happened. He tried again, pulling even harder, but still no luck. The skiff was too heavy. He'd have to attempt crossing hand over hand.

Dangling his feet over the bow, he cinched his backpack tighter, took a firm grip on the line and swung out over the water. Before he could hook his legs around the line, the skiff dipped into the trough of a wave. The line slackened and the lower half of his body plunged into the icy water. His boots filled and the added weight threatened to tear him off the line.

A second later, the line pulled taut again and he was jerked skyward. He kicked his feet wildly in the air before swinging them up and around the line. Water poured out of his boots and ran up his pant legs and under his coat, drenching his torso. He was safe. He dangled on the thick line, drew in a determined breath and pulled himself toward the *Black Skull*.

Inch by inch, hand over hand, he made his way up the line. The cold water froze his body, his hands became numb and his legs stung from the friction of the rough line. His sodden backpack felt like it weighed a thousand pounds as the straps dug painfully into his shoulders. The constant bobbing up and down was making him seasick.

This is not the slack line at the park.

He pushed the negative thoughts from his mind. His friend was in danger. He squeezed his eyes shut as tight as he could to keep out the salt water. The pain was excruciating but he pushed on.

When he was sure he couldn't possibly go another inch, he heard a loud, firm voice. "Come on, Murph! You can do this!"

Mr. Troutman? Coach Troutman, what are you doing here—

Murphy glanced from side to side. He'd heard his junior wrestling coach's voice plain as day.

"Come on, Murphy, keep going! Quitters are never winners! You can do this, you are strong. Come on, Murph! Don't give up, Katrina's counting on you."

Everything was blurry, he shook his head and blinked. His vision began to clear and he glanced around.

Am I delirious?

Murphy's hand hit something solid. He realized he was inches from a black mass.

I made it. I'm going to save Kat.

He reached through a scupper hole, grabbed a cleat and pulled himself closer to the stern. He heaved himself over the gunwale and onto the deck, flopping down like a landed salmon to lie gasping and sputtering. Murphy's heart beat so hard he feared someone would hear it. He rolled on his side and sucked in great gulps of air. His entire body ached.

After what seemed ages, his breathing normalized. His fingers stung, but feeling was returning. His eyes burned but he could see clearly. Rising on wobbly legs, he took a hesitant step. His knees buckled. Reeling, he slammed against the side of the cabin, lost his balance and fell to the deck.

They're going to hear me. I have to hide.

He quickly scanned the area and his eyes fell on a small hatch in the deck only a few feet away. He slithered toward it on his belly. It was small, only big enough to fit a slim man. Feeling was back in his fingers but they were hot and tingly and hard to control. He struggled to pull the release handle to undog the latch.

Murphy twisted and tugged with all his might. All of a sudden, the latch released and the cover came free in his hands. He heard a door slamming and raised voices.

Murphy hung on to the rim of the hatch so he would not slide away as the ship rolled in the waves. There was a momentary lull in the wind that let Murphy hear a familiar deep voice.

"What does he think is out here? I didn't hear anything, did you, Pew?"

"Nah, I didn't hear anything. Let's hurry and look around so we can get back inside where it's warm."

It's the Mickey Mouse guy.

"All right, I'm with you," said Bones. "But if there is someone out here, I'm going to plug 'em, and toss 'em overboard."

Murphy froze. He knew the man had a gun. Fear of discovery snapped him into action. Careful not to make any more noise, he scrambled through the opening, pulled the hatch cover back into place and dogged it down from inside. The handle was stiff and Murphy used all his strength. Just as he heard the latch click, the rusted piece of steel snapped off in his hands. He crouched silently as adrenaline coursed through him, staring at the useless piece of metal in his hand. He looked up at the cover. Heavy foot falls passed over his head and faded into the distance. Murphy surveyed his hiding place.

I'm trapped. This hatch is the only way out.

Chapter 23: Escape

He found himself in a small hold about half the size of his bedroom but half the height. It reeked of mildew. It was mostly empty but he saw a coil of line in the far corner and a stack of folded canvas sails sat against the fore bulkhead. His first assessment was correct: he was trapped. The hatch was the only way out. Trapped and frustrated, he knew he must get into the rest of the ship.

Now we both need saving.

He flexed his fingers. The feeling had returned, but they were still hot and stinging slightly, reminding him of the time he had frostbitten his ears during an ice fishing trip with his dad and Uncle Jerry.

He shivered uncontrollably. Murphy knew about hypothermia and its warning signs. Shivering was expected. If you no longer shivered or suddenly felt too warm, you definitely were in trouble. He knew he should stay moving to keep his blood flowing. His head throbbed and his knee ached and felt like it was still bleeding. He didn't look for fear of what he might find.

He stripped off his raincoat and sodden sweatshirt as well as his t-shirt. He wrung out both shirts before putting them back on. He wrung out his socks, ignoring his wet jeans before vigorously shaking out his coat and pulling it back on.

Why can I see?

He realized the hold was dimly illuminated, but there was no sign of a light fixture. There was a pale glow from the bottom of the far bulkhead behind the stack of canvas sails.

He stood and tested his legs, bent low so as to not hit his head, and took a shaky step. The motion of the ship threatened to throw him to the deck. His legs were wobbly but they supported him. He grabbed a wooden beam in the ceiling and hung on until he regained his balance, then staggered toward the illumination.

Approaching the bulkhead, he shoved aside the stack of musty canvas to reveal a rectangular hole the size of a math text book. The light came from somewhere within where someone had fastened two steel bars across the opening.

Murphy lay down on his stomach and peered through. He saw a much larger hold filled with boxes, crates, and mounds of what appeared to be camouflaged netting. A door in the far side of the room seemed to be the only way in or out. On a post in the center, an LED lantern hung from a rusty spike, swinging back and forth with the ship's motion.

Murphy's eyes followed the light down the post. He gasped. Directly below the lamp, Katrina sat tied to a four-legged metal chair. Her hands were lashed behind her with a thin cord. A dirty rag was wrapped around her mouth. Her face was red and her forehead was shiny with sweat. She was twisting, rocking back and forth, and straining at her bindings.

Murphy inspected the entire room and listened carefully. When satisfied Katrina was the only one there, he called in a low voice, "Kat, over here."

Her head whipped around and her eyes widened. She tried to speak but only managed a muffled groan through the rag. She struggled harder.

Murphy grabbed one of the two steel bars with both hands and pulled with all his strength. It didn't budge. He tried again, placing his feet on the bulkhead for leverage. Brute force wasn't working; there had to be another way. He examined the bars. At each end, a heavy screw fastened them to the wall.

I need a screwdriver.

He searched the tiny space, but found nothing except the sails and coils of line. He picked up the tee handle from the hatch but he couldn't see a way to use it. He rummaged through his sodden backpack and his pockets. In his jeans pocket, he found a dime. It fit the slot in the head of the screw but he couldn't get enough leverage to turn it.

He glanced at Katrina, whose eyes implored him. Murphy signed, "Don't worry, I'm coming." Along with most of their classmates, they had both learned American Sign Language in Mrs. Hill's social studies class after watching a documentary about Helen Keller.

He stripped off his belt and examined the buckle. There was a slot between the leather and the rest of the buckle. The slot fit neatly over the dime. He carefully applied pressure and the rusty screw began to turn. He focused intently on his task, ignoring the cramping in his hand.

The ship rocked violently in the waves jostling him from side to side. The roar of the wind and rain and spray splattering the deck above was deafening. Katrina continued to struggle in her attempt to free herself.

Finally, the first screw came loose enough so he could spin the last few turns with his fingers. He grasped the loose end of the bar with both hands and pulled. It bent an inch. He pulled harder bending it more. He repositioned his grip and placed a foot on the bulkhead and gave a mighty tug. The bar bent all the way back to the wall.

He quickly went to work on the other bar and the screw that fastened it.

Murphy watched as Katrina's chair tilted up on two legs. First on one side, then the other. The ship bucked fiercely and the chair flipped completely over, slamming her into a stack of crates. Katrina and the crates toppled to the deck with a cacophony of thuds and bangs. Murphy heard her grunt.

Forgetting she couldn't reply, he yelled. "Are you okay?"

Of course, he heard nothing from her but he saw her legs moving.

Did someone hear?

Sure enough, there were soon footfalls above. A few seconds later, the door flew open. Murphy ducked away just in time.

The door banged against the bulkhead. A man filled the opening.

"What's going on in here?" a deep voice boomed out. It was Bones.

Murphy slowly eased his eye to the edge of the hole and watched as Bones stepped through the doorway. The light glinted off the shiny silver pistol stuck in his belt. Bones rested an enormous hand on the tiny gun. The lamp illuminated his face. He had wild, curly brown hair, big bushy eyebrows, and a matted beard that reached halfway to his belt. His teeth were yellow and stained behind lips twisted into a permanent sneer. His eyes shifted back and forth as he sneered at Katrina.

Murphy gawked in awe and fear.

Even his beard is huge.

"So," Bones bellowed. "You're the one making all the racket. What do you think you're doing in here? You were trying to get loose, weren't you?"

He reached down with one hand, grabbed Katrina and the chair and effortlessly righted them.

"That wasn't very smart, was it? Just so you know, even if you get free, where yah gonna go? Better calm down, little girl, and behave yourself."

He gripped the butt of the pistol to make his point. He checked the knots and the gag before turning to leave. He reached the doorway and looked back. "You interrupt my poker game again, I won't be so nice."

Murphy locked eyes with Katrina and she rolled hers.

Acting tough like she's not scared. Maybe she isn't?

He desperately resumed work on the remaining screw. It wasn't as rusted as the first and after a few turns, he could remove it with his fingers. He immediately bent the remaining bar back, tossed his backpack through the opening and squirmed behind it, landing soundlessly on a coil of line. He snatched up his backpack, rushed to Katrina and pulled off the gag.

She took a few deep breaths and cleared her throat. "Th-thanks. What are you doing here? How did you get here?"

Murphy worked feverishly on the knots as he answered. "Saving you, what do you think?"

"Um, okay, thanks. Now who saves us?"

"Oh, we're good. I sent Hogan for help."

"What? What does that mean? Does he know where we are?"

He untied the last ropes. Katrina massaged her wrists as Murphy bent to work on the ropes around her feet. She bent to rub an ankle.

"I'll tell you everything later. Right now, let's get out of here."

She rose hesitantly on unsteady legs. "That giant heap of hair thinks he's tough when I'm tied to a chair and he's got a gun. We'll see what happens next time I see him."

"Settle down, Jane Wick, maybe a better idea would be escape before they keelhaul us."

"Either way."

Chapter 24: Topside

Heavy footfalls thumped and banged on the deck overhead. The ship shuddered and the constant rocking reduced in intensity. The roar of the wind dropped a few decibels but the rain continued its assault on the deck above.

There was a grinding noise, then a cough and a sputter. A constant hum started vibrating through the hull of the ship.

"They must have an inboard engine, too." Murphy whispered. "We need to get topside to see where we are."

He moved to the door. The handle turned with ease. He opened it a fraction of an inch and placed his eye to the slit.

He pulled his head back and whispered, "I saw a companionway at the end of this passageway. It must be the way up to the deck. Let's go."

He passed through the doorway and stepped quietly. Katrina stayed glued to his back. As they neared the companionway, a loud bang resounded over their heads. The ship shuddered and they froze.

The crash was followed by a low rattling that built in volume and speed until the entire ship shook. They heard a tremendous splash and the rattling soon stopped.

Murphy turned and climbed the rungs of a small ladder. When he reached the top, he eased open the hatch and peered into the dark. The noise from the wind and rain was overwhelming. Water splashed into his face. Lightning flickered in the distance and muted thunder boomed far off. Rain pounded the deck and the wind howled through the rigging as the ship groaned and creaked, swinging on its anchor.

Sounds like Davey Jones' ghost.

Katrina climbed up beside him for a quick glance. She wiped rain from her face and whispered, "They must have gone inside the main cabin. Let's get out of here."

Murphy pushed open the cover and scrambled onto the wooden deck. Katrina was close behind. He carefully closed the hatch cover and they squatted down next to the small shed.

Murphy could see they were on the foredeck of the *Black Skull* beside the anchor shed. Katrina nudged his arm and nodded toward the stern. He squinted through the rain. He saw the faint glow of light and realized it was shining through a porthole, dimly illuminating a portion of the deck. Shadows bounced off the bulkheads inside the cabin as darkened figures passed in front of the light. The rest of the deck was shrouded in gloom.

"Let's see if we can get to the stern and get into the skiff," Murphy said. "We'll have to sneak by the cabin."

He glanced about before he stood. The air suddenly exploded as lightning crackled nearby. For a second, everything was bright as day. Murphy glimpsed tall hulking trees looming overhead on the starboard side. High cliffs rose off the port side.

As quickly as it came the light disappeared, leaving him blinded. He blinked but his night vision was ruined. Even the cabin light was a faint blurry glow.

"I can't see." Katrina grabbed his arm.

"Me, either. We'll have to wait a minute."

They both cringed as a deafening explosion crashed overhead. They were caught in the open. Dangerously exposed.

Chapter 25: The Plank

They huddled together beside the anchor shed waiting for their vision to clear. Murphy was anxious and he felt Katrina shiver beside him.

He was starting to make out shapes when he heard a loud metallic click behind them, clear even over the din of the storm. Katrina's body jerked. They froze.

"Well," Carlson's voice boomed. "I see the detective boyfriend has arrived to save his fair maiden."

"He's not my boyfriend, yuck."

"We're cousins," Murphy blurted as they were suddenly bathed in light.

"Who cares who you are, you're trespassing on my ship. I could shoot you if I wanted. Trespassing is illegal and a man is allowed to protect his property." He let out a short, shrill laugh that pierced the wind. "Turn around real slow."

They both turned to face the tall, hooded man who stood before them holding a shotgun. He was back lit, his face obscured in shadows. Another, even bigger, man stood a few paces back. He was just a shape. But his size and long, flapping beard revealed his identity. Light reflected off the silver revolver he gripped in an enormous hand. He held a flashlight in the other.

Carlson raised his hood and took a step closer. He peered down his hawkish nose with penetrating, beady eyes. "So, little man, where did you come from and what are you doing on my ship?"

"I'm trying to help my cous—friend. And I might be a trespasser, but you're a kidnapper and a thief."

"We caught your, um friend, Little Miss Susie Q here," Carlson jerked his thumb at Katrina, "spying on me and my friends. Were you up there too, kid?" He scowled at Murphy. "Do you know what pirates do when they catch spies? They put them up in front of a firing squad. Isn't that right, Bones?"

"That's right, boss," grunted the giant. He stepped closer, revealing his shaggy face.

"It's not a war," Murphy snapped. "We're not spies. You're the spy. You spied on us and Isabelle."

"What happened to walking the plank? And you call your-selves pirates?" Katrina rolled her eyes and shook her head.

Murphy nudged her with his elbow.

"That's a fantastic idea. Of course, why didn't I think of that? You can walk the plank." Carlson leered at them. His pupils were magnified behind his rain-spotted glasses.

"Speaking of Isabelle. Where's the envelope she gave you? I saw her give it to you. And I heard rumors she found it in a safety deposit box her great granddad rented decades ago." He coughed into his hand. "Dang weather will be the end of me." He glanced up at the sky.

"Should I get a blindfold, boss?" Bones leaned closer to Carlson to be heard over the wind and rain. "And a sword? Do we have a sword, boss? I hope we have a sword."

Bones' long beard flapped in Carlson's face and he angrily swiped it away with his free hand. "Maybe later. But first, go get your bozo buddies. Then tie these two to the mast. Tie them tight. Hurry up. I'll keep them covered."

Bones passed his boss the flashlight and disappeared into the dark.

Carlson noticed Murphy grinning from ear to ear. "And what are you so happy about? Where's the letter?"

"I don't think you need to point a gun at us. We're kids and what could we do?" Murphy gestured around at the darkness. "And that thing isn't loaded and hasn't worked in a hundred years." He pointed at the shotgun. It was covered in rust and the stock had a piece missing.

Carlson glanced down at the double-barreled shotgun. He sneered and shrugged. "You got me, kid. I stole it from the museum. So, sue me. I like it for effect." He grinned but leaned the gun against the shed.

"Like you said, what you going to do, where you going to go?" He opened his arms and emitted a short coughing laugh.

Murphy's voice rose above the wind. "We know all about you and your crew. We know about your search for the gold, this fake pirate ship, and that you pretended to be a museum curator."

Carlson eyed Murphy. He swallowed, making his protruding Adam's apple bob erratically. "Maybe you're too smart for your own good, kid. Look where that got you."

Bones approached with a man on either side of him. Their faces were hidden in the shadows of their hoods. The glow revealed one of them was the man with the bandaged hand. The shorter man grabbed Murphy roughly by the shoulders and marched him toward the mast. He appeared muscular; his jacket was tight on his arms. He wore a black gator over his nose and mouth. When a gust of wind flung back his hood, Murphy saw the man's ears were misshapen.

Maybe he's a wrestler.

Bones picked Katrina up and carried her effortlessly under one arm. She squirmed and kicked but he seemed to hardly notice.

"Ouch! You big Sasquatch. Put me down."

He set her on the deck, grasped her arms with his massive hands and pushed her against the mast.

She kicked out, scraping the sole of her boot down his shin. He bellowed in pain and let go of her and she jumped aside lithely. As Bones bent over to rub his shin, she instantly drove her shoulder into his sternum. The big man grunted, released an explosion of air and slowly sank to one knee.

Murphy watched in awe and alarm as Katrina's slight frame was dwarfed by her immense adversary. He was relieved when she calmly stepped around the gasping man and casually bumped him with her hip. Bones teetered like a massive redwood felled by a logger's axe. He hit the deck with a resounding shudder, sprawling like a freshly-landed halibut. His mouth opened and closed as he tried to fill his lungs.

Katrina looked down at the beaten man and shook her head. She smiled and walked to the mast, turned and did a deep curtsy.

"Told you." She smiled demurely.

Murphy shook his head in wonder.

"Get them tied up tight, men," Carlson yelled.

Murphy whispered close to Katrina's ear. "Where did you learn how to do that? He must be five times your size."

"Videos."

"What?"

"Videos. They've been around a long time, you should check them out."

"I know what videos are. I'm just trying to figure out how you learned that from watching. Oh, just never mind."

The man with the lamp approached and Murphy saw it was Pew, the same man who had attacked him at his home. He carried a coil of yellow line.

"Hi, Mickey Mouse." Murphy grinned.

Pew lowered his head and silently assisted the stocky man. They roughly stripped the pack from Murphy's back and tossed it aside. The two men quickly had Murphy and Katrina tied firmly to the mast with their hands bound behind their backs and a long line coiled around their torsos and the mast.

"Y-you didn't bring the beast, d-did you?" Pew stuttered.

Carlson yelled, "Pew, Gunn, get below and grab the camo netting."

The stocky man called Gunn tugged on the ropes one more time. Bones slowly rose to his feet beside Carlson. Murphy noticed his face was contorted in pain. The big man shook his head as if to clear it. Water sprayed from his long beard.

Carlson scoffed. "Go help them, tough guy."

Bones glowered at Katrina. She smiled radiantly and batted her eyelashes.

Gunn and Pew emerged from below deck with armloads of camouflage netting.

Katrina whispered. "Where's the other guy? The one on this ship the first night?"

Before Murphy could reply, Carlson yelled over the storm. "Get it strung up, men. And hurry, I want everything squared away fast. Once I get what I need from these two, we'll have the last piece of the puzzle."

The men went to work spreading the netting over the entire ship. Murphy felt a slight vibration on the ropes that tied his wrists.

Carlson approached his prisoners. "I'm going to need that map you got from the lawyer's great-granddaughter. It's the map to the gold, isn't it? Tell me where it is. I'm done playing games."

"It wasn't a map and if it was, it's not like I would bring it with me. I'm not stupid," Murphy challenged.

"Bring his backpack."

The wind sang through the rigging but the boat's movement was minimal. Rain continued to pelt the deck in a chaotic rhythmic frenzy.

Carlson leaned closer to Murphy. "I know it was a map or you wouldn't have known where we were digging tonight, smarty pants."

Pew limped into the flashlight beam and handed Murphy's backpack to Carlson who started to unzip the first pocket.

"It's in my inside coat pocket. Go ahead and take it. It won't do you any good."

Katrina struggled to turn her body so she could look at Murphy. "What are you—"

Murphy twisted so he could see her and shook his head, then he addressed Carlson. "You already dug at the spot marked on the map. It is obviously not there and probably never was."

"Ah ha! It is a map. You're not so smart, huh, kid?"

Carlson tore open Murphy's rain jacket and retrieved the envelope from the water-tight pocket.

"Why did you bring— " Katrina began.

Murphy interrupted. "I forgot I had it."

"Pew, bring the lantern."

Pew appeared with the lantern and stood close to his boss.

"Set it down, dummy, go help."

Pew set the lantern on the slick deck and shuffled away into the gloom.

"I knew we were close." Carlson knelt on one knee beside the lantern and opened the envelope, shielding the pages with his body. "I knew it!" he yelled triumphantly. "We were in the right spot tonight. We would have found it if girlfriend over there didn't spook us." He glared at Katrina.

She smiled back. "Bunch of tough pirates scared off by little old me."

The three crewmen appeared around Carlson. "All done, boss," Bones rumbled.

Murphy glanced around the ship. The men had covered most of the vessel with the netting. They huddled around the lantern as Carlson showed them the map.

"What are you doing?" Katrina whispered.

"Just wait," Murphy whispered back. Momentarily distracted by the vibrations in his bindings, he paused.

Carlson pointed at the map. "It shows the gold is directly under this big tree. Do you remember a tree that was bigger than the others?"

The men murmured their ignorance. No one remembered seeing an especially big tree above the creek bank. "No, boss, I was looking at the ground, not the trees."

Pew nervously glanced over his shoulder. "You, you think he brought it?" he stammered.

"Who brought what?" Carlson asked.

"Th-the devil beast. You think the kid brought it?" Pew's eyes bulged in fear.

"It was a dog, you fool." Carlson turned away.

"Hey, boss, the tree where I found that violent little girl was huge. I don't know if it was the biggest though. They were all big up there."

"Good, at least one of you had your eyes open. But wrong side of the creek, dummy." Carlson tucked the map inside his coat and turned toward Murphy and Katrina. "I can't believe you two geniuses delivered the map right to me." He laughed at his prisoners.

"I'm not a good man," he said, leaning close to his captives. "But I'm no killer. There won't be a firing squad or a plank walking. Although I do see the poetry in such an endeavor."

Murphy watched as rivulets of water ran through Carlson's stubble and dripped off of his chin. Again, he felt the small vibration.

Katrina glared at Carlson. "You're only a thief, a liar, a burglar, a pickpocket, a vandal, and an actual kidnapper. So, there's like one thing you're not?"

Murphy felt the anger and revulsion in her tone. He knew not to interrupt when she was mad. Plus, he knew she didn't need his help.

Carlson seemed to understand he would not win an argument with her so he said nothing back and turned to address his men. "As soon as my boss gets here, we're heading back to finish digging. When we get the gold, we're clearing out of town."

He turned to Murphy and Katrina. "After we're safely away, I'll put in an anonymous call to the Coast Guard and tell them where you two are. That's the only way this is going to work."

The clouds thinned briefly; a beam of moonlight pierced through the small opening instantly lighting everything. Murphy saw the *Black Skull* was anchored at the head of a tiny lagoon. He saw the shore and the tall trees off the port side. And noticed a dense fog bank, rapidly approaching on the starboard before the light faded.

Carlson continued, "At the most, you two might miss a couple of meals and get a little wet. Better hope the ravens and eagles aren't hungry around here."

"You can't leave us out here. We'll get hypothermia or pneumonia and we can't last long without water." Katrina complained.

Murphy had just enough wiggle room in his bindings to bump her shoulder with his own. She snapped her head toward him, her eyes questioning. Murphy slowly shook his head. A sly smile spread across his face.

Carlson looked skyward and laughed. "I guess you'll have to open your mouth and drink rain. Besides I wouldn't worry, you two are pretty tough for a couple of brats."

Carlson leaned close. Even with the wind, Murphy could smell cigarettes on the man's breath. "There you go again, kid. You really must think this is a joke. I said I wasn't a killer. I can't say the same for some of my guys. After all, they are pirates."

"No, sir," Murphy said. "I don't think it's a joke. I think it's very real. When's your boss getting here? Are you sure he didn't get lost?"

Carlson stared at Murphy for a long minute. "You think you're pretty smart, don't you, kid?"

Murphy continued to smile, knowing it aggravated Carlson. "I know three things. One, you're not the brains, you're only the zookeeper." He looked at the other gang members. "Two, I'm betting there's someone a lot older and wiser leading this group. And three, I know you will never find the gold."

The wind's direction momentarily changed. It carried a noise that ebbed and flowed between gusts. It became recognizable as the chug of an engine coming from the opposite end of the lagoon, deep within the fog bank. The sound gained in volume as everyone turned to look.

Carlson yelled to his men, "Get a line ready, here he comes. Bones, get these two blindfolded, right now."

Bones towered over Murphy. In one hand, he held a dirty shirt, in the other, a double-edged knife. A distant bolt of lightning reflected off the blade as he raised it inches from Murphy's face.

Murphy was momentarily terrified and Bones saw it in his eyes and chuckled. He used the knife to cut the shirt into two strips. He pulled the cloth tight and tied it behind their heads. "You two keep your traps shut or I'll be back to show you how good I am at skinning."

A few minutes passed as the motor neared. Murphy felt a jolt as the *Black Skull* rocked gently.

He heard a shuffling of feet on the deck and the murmur of voices. He realized the wind was slacking and the downpour was less intense.

"Don't freak out," Murphy whispered to Katrina.

"Do you know who that is?"

"I've got a pretty good idea."

Chapter 26: Confession

"You should have listened to me, kid." A familiar voice resounded over the clamor of the weather. Katrina jolted beside Murphy and the vibration Murphy had been feeling stopped.

"I told you geology was a better pursuit. Now look what you got yourself into." The voice came closer to Murphy and abruptly, his blindfold was removed.

Ned Fisher stood before them. The edges of his dark brown poncho fluttered in the wind. A yellow sou'wester hat was pulled down low over his eyes, raindrops falling from the brim.

Murphy stared at the portly, bespeckled, elderly man and immediately noticed the day-old white stubble covering his face, the dark bags under his eyes, and his red nose.

"We don't need this." Fisher reached out and tugged off the dirty rag wrapped around Katrina's head. "Hello, Katrina. I should have known you were involved."

"Mr. Fisher," she sneered. Disgust dripped from her tone.

"You know these two?" Carlson questioned.

"Oh, yes, Murphy and I go way back. Say it's been eleven years now, right Murph?"

"Twelve. And it's Murphy."

"Now don't be like that, son."

"You're not my dad."

"What's he doing here?" Katrina asked.

"He's the one behind the whole thing."

"I wasn't surprised when Mr. Carlson called and described you." Fisher turned and addressed Carlson. "The boy's dad worked for me years ago. We're like family, right, son?"

"We're not family anymore. Untie us right now."

"I'm afraid you will have to stay tied up a little longer, but don't worry, you'll be found soon. We'll send someone to free you as soon as we get the gold and get out of town. I would like to sincerely thank you both for delivering the map. That was exceedingly nice of you." He lifted his head and laughed loudly.

Fisher spread his arms and gestured around. "What do you think of our hideaway? I discovered it years ago while working with some map makers. I always knew it would come in handy someday."

He pointed down. "The first *Black Skull* lies right below us on the floor of the lagoon."

He looked about at the other men. "By the way, as I'm sure you have surmised, these gentlemen work for me. You've met Mr. Carlson." He nodded at the tall man. "And there's Pew." He placed his hand on the thin man's shoulder. "Hogan and Murphy met him the other night." He indicated the hatchet-faced man with the bandaged hand. Pew glanced about nervously.

Fisher paused a moment before continuing his introductions. "I do have to apologize to you, Murphy. I thought you would be with friends or the neighbors that night. It's not my habit to terrorize children. Although these last few days, you've proven you're not a child anymore.

"That's Bones." He continued his introductions, nodding toward the giant bearded man with the revolver. "I guess you know him by now."

Then he pointed at the last man. "That's—"

"Yeah-Yeah, he's Gunn, we know already and who cares about their plagiarized names? You sound like a bunch of little boys playing make believe. What's your alias, Mr. Fisher? Wait, I Know. You're Long John Silver." Katrina laughed.

Pew's nasal whine rose over the wind. "How come he's telling them our names, boss? It's bad enough they've seen our faces."

"Is Pew your real name, dummy? Maybe read a book once in a while." Carlson shook his head in disgust.

"Get away from me," Carlson growled.

Murphy tested his bindings but found they were tight. He noticed the rain had settled into a light drizzle and the wind had slackened to a strong breeze. The moon shone behind a thinning layer of clouds providing a dim glow. Then he felt the vibration again.

Is the mast vibrating? Something running?

He spoke loudly. "How long have you been a criminal, Mr. Fisher? What happened to you?"

Fisher stepped closer. "I hardly see myself as a criminal. I've done nothing wrong. I just hired these fine gentlemen to dig a few holes on some private property."

He looked around at the men. "As far as I can tell, that gold is public property. No one can prove who it belongs to at this point. Even though your relative buried it, he stole it in the first place. "

"We don't want any favors from you." Murphy spoke with conviction. "And I think trespassing, vandalism, kidnapping, attempted burglary, and assault all fall under the 'you're a criminal' category."

"Your family has no more claim to it than I do, Murph. If you can get over yourself, maybe we can work this out. We can cut you in for a share." Murphy watched as Fisher's eyebrows bounced up and down as he talked. They had always reminded him of big, hairy, gray caterpillars.

"They're not getting any of mine," Carlson grumbled.

"Not mine," repeated Bones.

Pew and Gunn muttered their displeasure as well.

"Looks like it'll have to come out of your end, Ned," Carlson said.

"I don't see why we have to cut them in anyway. Let's leave them here for the birds."

Fisher stared at Murphy for a long time.

"We have to go, boss." Carlson's voice snapped him out of his revery. "We can't miss this tide or we're not getting out of here."

Fisher broke eye contact with Murphy. He shrugged his shoulders. "Fine, Murph, have it your way. Stubbornness runs in your family." He turned away.

"It's Murphy. What happened to you? Why are you doing all this?"

Fisher looked back. "I'm broke, son. I'm about to lose my house. I have medical bills. I just want to enjoy the rest of my life." His lower lip quivered.

He removed his sou'wester and ran his hand through thinning snow-white hair. "I've been finding tidbits of info on the *Black Skull* for years. Eventually, I put most of it together. After Edna died, there was nothing holding me back. I hired Carlson here to take the museum job and search for the missing details."

Murphy noticed the other men were gathered by Fisher's launch, the *Edna*.

"I spent the last of my money on this old tub and rigging it out to look more like a pirate ship, like the original *Black Skull*. I found it in a boat yard in Bremerton, Washington. She was an original Puget Sound fishing boat when wind was the only power needed. Someone later added the engine. It comes in handy."

Fisher jerked his thumb toward the other men. "When Carlson discovered Florence's journal, we hired the others." He shook his head. "Not a sailor among the bunch."

"You figured if it worked once, it would work again, huh?" Murphy glared at the old man. A not-so-distant clap of thunder made them all flinch.

"Exactly, son. If it worked for Larson and Blackwell, it would work for us."

"Not your son."

Fisher ignored the comment. "This *Black Skull* is much smaller but it does the trick, doesn't it, Murph? It sure fooled you."

"Did it?" Murphy smiled.

"That was you on the *Black Skull* that first night, wasn't it?"

"Boss?" Carlson's voice interrupted.

Fisher turned toward the men.

"You'll never find it," Murphy called.

Fisher glanced at Carlson. "You've got the map, right?"

Carlson nodded and tapped his breast pocket. "Yes, sir. All we have to do is locate the biggest tree on the south bank and dig directly under it."

Fisher looked back to Murphy. "The map tells us, son."

"But does it really?" Murphy noticed the vibration in his binding had intensified.

Fisher coughed out a short laugh. "Yes, I think it really does."

"We'll see."

Fisher shook his head and turned away. "All right, boys, before the night's out, we'll all be rich. We'll pull *Edna* right up on the beach at the mouth of Anderson Creek. Even if someone sees us, the gold is ours. No one is taking it from us. Besides, my boat will out run any other."

Murphy felt the vibration stop as Katrina spoke.

"I guess the saying is right. Gold does make people greedy jerks." She twisted her body and Murphy felt the vibration return.

"Is that how it goes?" Murphy asked.

"Close enough," she replied.

Fisher's eyes passed over Katrina and he turned away from them.

"You wouldn't find it even if you have the chance to dig for it," Murphy called to Fisher's back.

"You're a pretty smart kid, Murphy, but you don't know everything."

Carlson offered his arm and Fisher grasped it to steady himself as he stepped from the *Black Skull* onto the *Edna*.

"Don't worry, you won't be here long," Fisher called from his boat.

"We know," Murphy yelled back.

Chapter 27: Rage in the Rigging

Katrina and Murphy watched as the men situated themselves on the *Edna.* Fisher fired up the engine and they started to pull away.

Suddenly, Murphy felt the lines encircling his body release. He was caught off balance and nearly fell forward.

I'm free.

He turned toward Katrina. She was shrugging off ropes. "Oops, that was a bit premature."

Her hood was thrown back and her fuchsia locks were plastered to her head. Her hands were free and she held a red pocket knife with a white cross. She was grinning.

Murphy gazed in wonder.

Lock picks, ninja outfit, pickpocketing, beating up grown men. Who is she?

Katrina reached out and spun him around. In seconds, she had sawed through the line that secured his wrist.

"Run!" he yelled and spun toward the aft of the *Black Skull* and the smaller skiff.

Murphy skirted the main cabin and jumped over a pile of crates. His head scraped the low netting. He glanced over his shoulder to be sure Katrina was on his heels as he heard a yell from the *Edna.*

He reached the aft cleat and fumbled with the thick line. As soon as it was loose, he began pulling the skiff toward the *Black Skull.* The heavy skiff barely moved. Katrina crouched beside him and, hand over hand, she helped him pull.

The yelling grew louder as the bow of the *Edna* came into view. Fisher was at the helm. He held the engine at idle but they were approaching fast.

"We can't beat them; we have to try something else."

"I'm not jumping in," Katrina replied calmly.

"Climb the mast." His voice was fast and loud and he didn't wait for an answer but turned and ran toward the center of the ship. They arrived at the mast at the same time.

Murphy heard the *Edna* bump into the *Black Skull* with a resounding clunk. Voices rose and footsteps landed on the deck.

Katrina sprang at the mast and was at the first yardarm in a flash. Murphy followed and was soon standing beside her. They both hugged the thick mast. They were approximately fifteen feet above the deck. The horizontal wooden arm was slippery and they struggled to stand on it.

They watched as the men gathered below and saw the fury on their faces. Only Fisher's face was blank. Murphy thought he looked sad.

Fisher's voice rose above the rest. "Leave them be, men. What can they do, where can they go? Let's board up and go get the gold."

"I'm not leaving these two meddling snoops running around loose until I get my hands on the gold." Carlson shot back.

Fisher moved away from the group. The rest of the men stood staring at Carlson.

"Sorry, Ned." Carlson spoke. "These men work for me." He pointed at Gunn. "Go get them."

Murphy felt Katrina squeeze his arm. She gestured up with her eyes. He nodded and she rapidly shimmied up the mast to the second yardarm. He glanced below and watched the stocky man called Gunn begin to climb.

Murphy saw Gunn slip and nearly fall before grunting in frustration and resuming his ascent. Gunn flung a wet arm over the yardarm inches from Murphy's boots. Long, white fingers reached for his leg. "Come here, punk," the man with the cauliflower ears growled.

Pale fingers clutched at air as Murphy raised his foot and stomped down hard. He felt his boot catch two of them under his heel.

A scream pierced the night. Murphy dropped to the yardarm, straddled it and shimmied outward from the mast and away from the howling man. When he reached the end, he stood and grasped the forestay running from the yardarm to the upper arm then to the top of the mast.

Gunn spewed a string of threats and alternately shook his hand and sucked on his fingers.

The men below watched in silence as Gunn eventually climbed to his feet. He looked up where Katrina stood, then back at Murphy.

"Come out here and get me, tough guy," Murphy taunted.

Gunn scowled and looked down before hesitantly scooting toward Murphy. He made slow progress. The yardarm was slippery and it was obvious his hand hurt. He wobbled as he inched closer.

"Climb, Murphy," Katrina's voice rang out.

Gunn abruptly scrambled the last few feet and lunged at Murphy who bent his knees slightly and leapt upward, fingers grabbing the forestay. He wound his legs around the thick line and scurried skyward. For a moment, Gunn held onto his boot but Murphy kicked free and ascended rapidly.

A tight slack line. Easy.

Murphy quickly reached the end of the upper yardarm and clung to the forestay that continued to the top of the mast.

Glancing down, he saw Gunn scooting back toward the safety of the mast.

The stocky man was obviously past being cautious and moved rapidly. He reached the mast and stood, then immediately began climbing toward Katrina.

Murphy watched helplessly as Gunn closed in and lunged. Like a cat, Katrina leapt out of the way and effortlessly ran across the glistening upper yardarm to its tip. Katrina didn't slow down but grabbed the forestay with both hands and swung her body completely around in a graceful arch, landing both feet on the slender wooden pole.

Show off.

"We're wasting time here, leave them alone. Let's go." Fisher's voice rose from below.

Gunn was determined and began scooting toward Katrina.

Murphy took a few quick steps across the upper yardarm. Reaching the mast, he hugged it. Now he was behind Gunn who was closing in on Katrina.

Without a thought, Murphy sprang away from the mast and ran across the glistening yardarm toward Katrina and Gunn.

Katrina teetered on the tip, clinging to the forestay and kicking at the stocky man. Murphy slammed onto Gunn's back and he fell forward, his face smacking the wooden pole with a resounding clonk. Murphy's momentum carried him over the prone man and toward the deck below. At the last second, he grabbed the forestay next to Katrina.

The coarse rope burned his palms and he involuntarily let go, screaming in agony and fear. "Noooooo!"

A hand seized his wrist. For a moment, he was weightless, his body swinging out over the darkened void in a great arc. Then he crashed into Katrina. The collision nearly knocked them both from their slippery perch. They clutched each other and the forestay, desperate to keep their balance on the narrow pole.

He looked down to see Gunn swinging under the yardarm. His fingers were locked together over the pole. His eyes bulged in fear and blood gushed from his nose. Murphy and Katrina watched as his pale fingers slipped a fraction of an inch.

"Help me," Gunn implored. But his grip released and he disappeared into the dark. A blood curdling scream was instantly followed by a tremendous splash.

For a long moment, there was only the sound of the wind and rain.

"Get him out of there!" Fisher yelled.

Murphy looked below. He saw Carlson's pale face turn upward. For a moment, their eyes locked. Murphy nodded and smirked.

Carlson shook his head and turned away. He gestured to the men and they began reboarding the *Edna*. Before he boarded, Carlson cut the painter of the small skiff. Murphy and Katrina watched helplessly as it slowly drifted away from the stern of the *Black Skull*.

"I'm glad they're leaving, but not looking forward to staying here until who knows when."

Murphy cocked his head, "Did you hear that?"

She wasn't listening. "That and the fact that those jerks get all the gold. I'm just saying. What? Hear what?"

"Don't worry. They aren't going far and they're not getting the gold. Didn't you hear it?"

"Hear what? All I hear is the rain and wind."

Fisher took his place at the helm and Carlson plopped down in the opposite seat. The wet and disgruntled Gunn shoved off with a boat hook and the antique launch floated away from the *Black Skull*. The engine kicked over and rumbled to life.

Katrina and Murphy were left alone in the gloom. "Let's go down." Murphy turned toward the mast.

Chapter 28: Deadly Armada

Fisher and the men were only a few yards off the starboard side and moving slowly. Fisher kept the *Edna* at idle, concerned about reefs in the ebbing tide.

"There it is again, did you hear it?" Murphy asked as they stood on the deserted deck of the *Black Skull.*

"What? It sounds like a dog barking. Is that what you're talking about?"

Before Murphy could reply, a massive geyser erupted near the bow of the *Edna.* The concussion and rush of water violently rocked the launch, nearly spilling Gunn and Pew into the lagoon. The men grabbed onto whatever they could, including each other. Water cascaded down on the launch.

Even the *Black Skull* rocked on its anchor. Murphy and Katrina steadied themselves and gawked in astonishment.

A deafening boom resounded across the lagoon, echoed off the trees, and rumbled along the peaks of the nearby mountain tops. As the roar faded, a bright light illuminated the fog bank, casting a dim glow across the lagoon.

The barking intensified in volume but was quickly drowned out by an amplified voice. "Gentlemen in the launch," a woman's voice cut sharply through the wind and rain. "Stay where you are or I'll fire again." Slightly muffled, she added, "I've always wanted to say that."

"Mrs. Sutter?" Katrina blurted.

"In case any of you are wondering, that was a 50mm howitzer round, complete with a high explosive tip for maximum damage. As I think we have already demonstrated, accuracy is not an issue, so I suggest you boys in the motor launch throw your weapons overboard and get your hands up.

"Do it now!"

"Definitely, Mrs. Sutter." Katrina spoke.

"And Hogan, can't you hear him?" Murphy asked.

"Reload, ladies! Draw a bead and be ready to fire."

"Hogan? How did he get here? What's happening?"

"Okay, okay!" Fisher yelled. "Calm down there—Diane—Diane Sutter, is that you?"

"Shut up, Ned, and do what you're told. Do it now!"

"I told you Hogan went for help." Murphy laughed.

Fisher and the men seemed to be racing each other to get their hands up. Carlson tossed the broken shotgun overboard and nodded to Bones who rummaged to retrieve his revolver. In his haste, he accidentally elbowed Pew, sending him reeling over the side into the black, frigid water.

Pew disappeared under the surface for a long moment but soon popped up, screaming and flailing his arms. "Help! I can't swim! Please!" He sputtered, gasped and disappeared a second time. Bones casually reached into the depths with one massive hand. He seized Pew by his hair, jerking him half out of the water with a mighty tug before dragging him over the rail like a sack of wet seaweed.

Pew curled into a ball at the men's feet. Between coughing fits, he moaned and whimpered about a devil beast with red eyes and razors for teeth.

"Throw the key overboard, too, Ned," Mrs. Sutter's scratchy voice blared.

Fisher pulled the keys from the ignition and reluctantly tossed them into the water. Murphy noticed the *Edna* was slowly drifting back toward the *Black Skull.*

"Hogan and Mrs. Sutter are rescuing us and blowing up stuff? That makes sense. Not," Katrina puzzled.

"Well, I did send Hogan for help but I have no idea why he's here now with Mrs. Sutter."

As they watched, the boat full of sullen thieves drifted slowly back. A number of small vessels nosed their way through the fog bank and entered the lagoon. Their running lights cast a green and red glow on the water.

Suddenly a single bright light illuminated *Edna* and Fisher's men and the *Black Skull.*

Murphy and Katrina blinked rapidly; their eyes unaccustomed to light revealing a tiny lagoon hardly large enough for the *Black Skull* to turn about. On three sides, cliffs rose out of the water and towered overhead. Snow-tipped mountains stood like disapproving sentinels behind them. The entrance to the lagoon was a narrow opening in the rocky shoreline obscured by tall spruce trees.

Murphy counted five boats cautiously approaching. "Murphy, Katrina, are you okay?" his mother's voice boomed over the speaker. "Are you hurt? Hold on, I'll be right there."

Murphy and Katrina glanced at each other. Murphy shrugged.

The boat with the powerful light drew closer. Murphy saw it was a twenty-foot runabout with a wide beam and a large foredeck, a popular design in Southeast Alaska. He was relieved to see his mom on the bow. She was wrapped in a bright yellow poncho and her long, black hair flapped as she leaned into the wind. She brushed it away from her eyes.

Diane Sutter was standing beside her and between them Hogan bounced up and down. He was barking and shaking his rump so hard it almost sent him overboard with each tail wag.

An aluminum seine skiff pulled alongside them with two women hunched over a small cannon mounted to the bow.

It's the cannon from Mrs. Sutter's desk at the museum.

Mrs. Sutter had a bull horn in one hand and a harpoon in the other. She lowered the bull horn but spoke loudly. "Keep it aimed right at them, ladies. I don't trust these guys. If they make a move, blow them out of the water."

"Diane, w-what the—" Fisher stuttered.

"Shut up, Ned," Mrs. Sutter hollered.

More boats approached Fisher's drifting launch, surrounding him and the gang. Each boat held two or three women and many held a shotgun or rifle trained on Fisher and his men. The boats merged, gently bumping Fisher's launch, pinning the *Edna* to the hull of the *Black Skull*.

When Mrs. Sutter's boat was still feet away from the *Black Skull*, Murphy's mom hurdled the void and landed on the deck of the *Black Skull*. She was followed by an ecstatic Hogan. They both rushed to Murphy and Katrina.

Mrs. Sutter boat bumped the *Black Skull* and she threaded her bow line through the rail, snubbing it fast to a deck cleat.

Sonia gathered Murphy and Katrina in her arms and squeezed them with all her strength. Murphy felt something hard at her waist under the poncho and guessed it was his dad's hand gun.

Katina felt it also and raised her eyebrows. Murphy shrugged and smiled.

Hogan put his paws on Murphy's chest and licked his face furiously. Murphy laughed. For once, he didn't mind.

Sonia hugged and kissed them. Murphy was shocked when he noticed Katrina laughing.

I thought she hated hugs.

Finally, Sonia released them and stood up, one arm on each of their shoulders.

"That's enough, you serial licker." Murphy pushed Hogan away. "I wasn't worried, Mom. I knew you and Hogan would find us. No idea how, but I'm sure glad you did."

Hogan jumped up on Katrina and licked her face. "Get down, Hoge." She pushed him away. His spirits where not dampened as his rear end gyrated in circles as he wiggled between their legs. He licked any unguarded hand.

Sonia spoke. "When Hogan showed up outside my bedroom window, my heart sank. I quickly realized you two were gone and guessed where you went and why." She glared at Murphy. "We will talk about that later." She looked from face to face. "Seriously, I died for a minute tonight. Never do that to me again." She squeezed their shoulders.

They winced but were quiet. Katrina glanced sideways at Murphy. He grimaced. Sonia released her grip.

They turned to survey the small armada of boats and armed women. Katrina spread both arms and gestured. "How did all this happen?"

"Hogan showed up all muddy and slobbery and I found the note on his collar."

"What exactly did Murphy say in that note?"

Mrs. Sutter's piercing voice interrupted them. "Okay, men, one at a time, you're going to step onto my boat."

Murphy recognized the twin sisters who taught at his school. They were crouched in an aluminum skiff on the other side of the *Edna*. They both had stern looks on their faces and both held a shotgun in the curve of their arms.

"These nice women," Mrs. Sutter nodded at Linda and Sarah Connolly, "they'll keep you covered while Helen and Sandra tie you up."

She indicated two more women who stood in the rear of her own boat. One held a coil of line and the other had a deck knife in her hand. "I'm sure you'll enjoy it as it seems you don't mind tying up children."

Murphy recognized the women wearing long rain jackets. The one in red was Helen Parks who owned a popular restaurant in Douglas and the slender woman in green was Sandra Evans who with her husband, Phil, ran the outboard shop on the Back Loop.

"Tie those knots tight. Let's see how they like it," Mrs. Sutter instructed. "Cooperate and do what you are told. Just so you know, all these women have black belts in Judo. They won't have any problem breaking your arm or throwing you into the drink."

Mrs. Sutter motioned toward a woman crouched low in the bow of a nearby aluminum skiff. The woman braced a shotgun against the gunwale and pointed it at the men. A shock of red hair poked out beneath a wool cap. The woman's gaze never left the men.

"Maeve, over there." Mrs. Sutter gestured at the red-headed woman. "She's a three-time state champion trap shooter and my friend, Lucile, over there." She pointed at a dark green Freighter canoe where a small woman dressed entirely in black stood expertly holding a large compound bow with the string drawn back. "Lucile just completed her second successful solo grizzly bear bow hunt on Kodiak Island. I wouldn't try her."

Gunn stepped from the *Edna* to Mrs. Sutter's runabout. Helen Parks pulled his hands behind him. Sandra Evens tied them and then made him sit cross-legged on the deck.

Sandra used a deck knife to cut another length of line from the coil. "You are next, Ned. I always knew there was something slippery about you."

Fisher hesitantly stepped onto Mrs. Sutter's boat with the help of Carlson's arm. Fisher managed to keep his hands up high, but his head was down, his chin was buried in his chest. He didn't look at anyone as he moved slowly on shaky legs.

Murphy stood beside his mom. Katrina stood on her other side. Sonia had her arms around them. She squeezed and pulled them close.

The women tied Fisher's hands and feet and helped him sit down on the deck beside Gunn.

Then it was Bones' turn. Sarah cut another length of line and handed it to Helen. They stood ready for the immense man.

When Bones stepped onto Mrs. Sutter's boat, it settled noticeably in the water. He stood still in front of her. He loomed over her and scowled. Her eyes never left his and she showed no fear. In fact, Murphy though she looked bored.

In the flash of an eye, Bones lunged, his fat fingers stretching for her neck.

There was a blur of motion and suddenly the giant cartwheeled in the air, his feet flew over his head, and he crashed violently to the foredeck with a sickening thud. It was as though he was caught in a sudden gust that tossed him like a dried leaf. His head bounced once, making the sound of wood hitting metal. He lay still.

Her small boat rocked violently. Gunn and Fisher bumped together. The three women showed superb balance and rode out the sudden explosion of motion with ease.

Diane Sutter stood where she had been before the attack. Murphy was amazed to see she still held the bull horn in one hand and the harpoon in the other. He shook his head and blinked rapidly.

What just happened here? How did she?

Katrina whooped in delight.

Mrs. Sutter gazed down at the heap at her feet. In a calm voice, she instructed the women, "Get him tied up." She turned to the remaining men. "Anyone else feeling frisky?"

"Girl power," Katina uttered quietly.

"Girl power," Sonia repeated.

Murphy rolled his eyes but smiled.

"Murphy, your note said you figured Ned Fisher was somehow involved, but how did you know?" Sonia asked.

"I didn't at first, but later I thought it was weird when he pretended not knowing anything about the *Black Skull* and he tried to steer me away from looking into it." Murphy wiped rain from his face.

"I mean it's not like there were no references to the boat at all. Carlson dug up some and Mr. Fisher has written three books about shipping and shipwrecks in Alaska."

Hogan continued to push between their legs and lick hands. On occasion, he barked in excitement.

"What we found at the museum proved he was lying for a reason." Murphy pushed back his hood and smoothed his hair. He noticed the rain had turned into a fine mist.

"Then I thought it was sus that Mrs. Sutter's husband saw him talking to Carlson at the harbor the day after Carlson was supposedly tending to a family emergency."

"And the fact Carlson was using Mr. Fisher's name when he talked to Isabelle," Katrina contributed.

"Yes, that too. It proved they knew each other. All the little things added up to his involvement."

Hogan stiffened and barked loudly. Pew was about to step onto Mrs. Sutter's boat.

Sonia spoke. "When I got the note, I knew explaining things to the police would be time consuming or worse, so I decided to call Diane. She's such a tough woman and smart, too. I knew she was still at the dojo instructing the late class. She often fills in for Sensi Malcom. I just knew she would help if she could."

Hogan growled and gnashed his teeth. Murphy held his collar. Hogan's eyes didn't leave Pew.

"I explained your note to her, Murph. Diane said her husband mentioned bumping into Ned only a few moments before. He said he saw him readying the *Edna* to leave; Ned seemed agitated and in a big hurry. Her husband thought it strange the elderly man was heading out into a storm at night by himself. But thought he was possibly going to visit a friend in Douglas only a short distance across the channel. Diane gathered the gals and I rushed to meet them at the Juneau boat harbor."

Murphy noticed it was Pew's turn to be tied up. The pathetic man stood alone on the *Edna's* bow, shivering and dripping. His arms were wrapped tightly around his quaking body and his eyes were glued to Hogan. His gang mates sat shoulder to shoulder in two tight rows in the bottom of Mrs. Sutter's skiff.

Murphy's mom spoke, "When I arrived at the harbor, I met Mrs. Sutter and the rest of the class. Fisher was pulling out in the *Edna*. We hurried to follow him. We kept all our lights off and communicated on a private channel on the VHF radio."

They all noticed Pew ignored Mrs. Sutter's commands and remained in place. But when one of the Connolly sisters poked him in the ribs with her shotgun, he hesitantly shuffled forward and raised his hands. His eyes were filled with fear and never left Hogan. He stood frozen, his arms up.

Hogan chose that second to lunge, catching Murphy by surprise as he broke from his grasp and rushed to the gunwale of the *Black Skull*. With forepaws on the rail, he barked and growled and gnashed his teeth.

Pew's face turned pale and his eyes bulged while his arms remained pointing to the sky. His feet began moving in an attempt to run, but for a moment, his body remained in place. Abruptly, he gained traction on the slippery deck and accelerated down the length of Diane's boat, running between and over his gang mates.

A blood-curdling scream erupted from his terrified lips. He didn't stop at the stern, but launched himself into the inky lagoon. Apparently choosing drowning over evisceration by the devil beast. Pew desperately kicked his feet and for a split second his upper body stayed out of the water. He reminded Murphy of a dolphin doing a tail dance.

Pew quickly sank beneath the obsidian surface. One of the small skiffs floated close and two of the women casually grabbed him by his hair and pulled him over the side of the skiff. They effortlessly tossed him into Mrs. Sutter's boat like a slab of meat. He blubbered like a baby as his hands were tied and he was positioned beside his sullen crewmates.

Mrs. Sutter easily hopped aboard the *Black Skull* and approached Murphy, Katrina and Sonia. "Hey there, youngsters. How did you like the cannon? Pretty cool, huh?"

"Pretty cool, for sure. It was totally awesome," Murphy blurted.

"I've been meaning to return it to the Coast Guard. It's been in my trunk for a few days so I thought why not bring it."

"Where did you learn to shoot it so accurately?"

Mrs. Sutter laughed. "I know how to shoot it because my husband is on avalanche patrol and they use something similar to knock down snow cornices. That's actually where I got the fifty-millimeter round. He keeps some locked in a strong box in our locker at the harbor." She leaned in close. "I only had the one." She smiled and put her finger to her lips. "I've been with my husband a number of times when he's fired it, but to be perfectly honest, the accuracy thing was a total fluke. I was trying to shoot over their heads. Over everyone's head for that matter."

Murphy glanced at his mom and Katrina as they both paled.

"So, what do we do now?" Katrina asked.

"I guess we better head back to town and call the police so we can get rid of these amateurs." Mrs. Sutter chuckled.

She turned toward her boat and stared at Carlson. "I always knew you were a slime ball, Carlson. From the day you stepped through the museum door, I had you pegged. I'm happy to see you'll get what's coming to you. People have got to learn to respect history. It's not something to play at. It's serious."

"Yeah, yeah, whatever," Carlson muttered to himself and looked down at his knees.

Chapter 29: Big Reveal

It was late morning the day after the gang's capture. Murphy and Katrina sat with Sonia at the breakfast bar in their kitchen.

A pot of tea sat on a pot holder beside honey and a tiny saucer with lemon slices. All three held cups and were cautiously taking small sips of the hot liquid.

"Lieutenant Burnett from the Juneau Police Department called me and gave me an update earlier."

"What did he say, Mom?"

"Carlson and his men are being charged with trespassing, property destruction, and kidnapping." She set her cup down and wiped her lips on a napkin.

"What about Mr. Fisher, Mom? What's will happen to him?"

"It's a little different for him because he didn't actually do the things Carlson and the others did. For now, he's being charged with collusion and conspiracy to commit kidnapping and unlawful detention."

A metallic clamor resounded from across the street, interrupting the hum of Mr. Wallace's mower. Sonia sprung from her stool and quickly closed the kitchen window.

"He's also being charged with fraud as it turns out he bought the ship that became the *Black Skull* under false pretenses. He used fake documents and didn't pay the owners."

Katrina shook her head. "I guess you never know about people. I always thought he was so nice." She paused a moment. "Something has been bugging me."

"What's that?"

"When we were on the *Black Skull*, you told Mr. Fisher they would never find the gold. Why did you say that? What makes you so sure they would never find it?"

"I've been waiting for someone to ask." Murphy smiled. "It wasn't because I was sure they'd be caught. I'm sure I know where the gold is and it's not on the Walkers' property."

"Really? Do tell, oh wise Sherlock. If it's not there, where is it?"

"Okay, Watson, here goes."

"Irene Adler."

"What?"

"I'm not Watson; he's old, big and slow. I'm Irene Adler, she kicks both their butts."

"Who?"

"From *A Scandal in Bohemia*."

"Oh, I haven't read that one."

"Not surprised."

"I read."

"Galaxy Phantom comic books don't count."

"You can learn a lot from them. Anyway, the map showed the X below a huge tree on the right bank of the creek and it looks like it's on the Walkers' property." Murphy sipped his tea.

He heard a faint metallic clang again. He smiled and continued. "The problem with that idea is there are at least seven huge trees above the creek on that side, and none that stand out as bigger than the others. On the other hand, Willy's Tree—"

"Who? What tree?" Sonia interrupted.

"Mom, you remember when Willy Spencer broke his collar bone?"

"Yes, I remember he fell out of ... oh, that's not nice. You kids are mean."

Katrina raised her hands. "Don't look at me."

"Of course not. Boys are mean."

Murphy shrugged. "Willy doesn't mind having a tree named for him. And for sure it is the biggest one anywhere around and much bigger than any of the trees on the Walkers' property."

"But you said their property and yours meet on the top of the ridge, couldn't it still be on their property?" Katrina asked.

"Either way it puts, er, Willy's Tree for no better name, on the wrong side of the creek according to the map," Sonia said.

"I've been thinking about that, Mom. Willy's Tree is on a ridge that separates our property from Anderson Creek. On the far side of the ridge is Anderson Creek and the flat bank where Carlson dug below the Walkers' house. On the other side of Willy's Tree and that wall of brush, it drops off to the beach. Right there." Murphy pointed out the side window.

They all turned to look.

"You can see Willy's Tree is the tallest on the ridge and that ridge overlooks that dry creek bed." He continued to point.

"Okay, yes, we walked across it the other night. I remember. So what?" Katrina asked.

"It wasn't always dry."

"What do you mean?" Sonia asked.

"Mom, you're the one who told me many of the creeks around here were diverted for various reasons in the past. Some for hydroelectric use in the mines and mills and some because they were in the way of a new construction."

"Yes, that's right, many of the creeks were diverted."

Murphy watched their faces as they comprehended what he was saying.

"Are—are you saying the gold is on this side of the tree by that dry creek on our property?" Sonia eyes were huge behind her glasses.

Murphy watched as her bangs fell in front of her face and she didn't swipe them away. He shifted his gaze to Katrina. She was absolutely still. Her eyes sparkled and the edges of her mouth twitched as she hopped off her stool, knocking it over in excitement.

Hogan startled, shot to his feet, got tangled in the spare stool and it also went flying.

"Hey, Mom, can we get a metal detector now?"

She rushed from the room. "I'm calling your dad."

"Should I order it?" he called after her.

Chapter 30: Where's the Gold?

Murphy woke to the sound of rain on the roof. He threw off his blanket and swung his feet to the floor. He glanced at the window.

It's early.

He was excited. This day had taken too long to arrive. He dressed quickly in jeans and a Galaxy Phantom hoodie.

Hogan stood up from his position on the floor beside the bed. He stretched and yawned as Murphy headed toward the kitchen. "Come on, sleepy."

Murphy felt a tiny twinge of annoyance when he saw Katrina sitting at the breakfast bar sipping lemon tea with honey. She perched on the stool like a bird hugging her knees.

"Couldn't sleep any longer, huh?"

"No and I didn't get a lot either." He glanced out the side window. "See anyone yet?"

"Nope, just you and muttly." Hogan licked her dangling hand. She pulled it back quickly.

She wore jeans and a crimson hoodie with bold white lettering emblazoned across the front: "Reality is wrong. Dreams are for real."

Murphy read it out loud, "Freud?"

"Tupac."

They were interrupted by an insistent beep-beep-beep. An orange light flickered across the walls.

Murphy rushed to the window. "He's here!" His voice was loud in the quiet house.

A large green truck towing a trailer with a small yellow excavator perched atop was parking on the street. The sign on the door of the truck read "Randy's Lawn and Sewer. I'm Down with Green or Brown."

Murphy rushed to the hallway and stuffed his feet into rubber boots. He flung on his rain slicker and headed out the door.

In a few minutes, he reentered the house. He hung up his jacket and kicked off his boots. He found his mom and dad with Katrina and Hogan in the kitchen. John was readying the coffee maker as Sonia sipped her tea.

"Mr. Green said he will be set up to dig in thirty minutes or so." Murphy swiped a hand at his wet bangs.

"This is so exciting," Sonia exclaimed.

"So, now you think it's there, Mom?"

"There's a good chance. I'll say fifty-fifty."

"I'll go seventy-thirty." John said.

"Hundred percent." Katrina and Murphy said at the same time.

"Jinx."

"There were times when I didn't think we would ever get to this day," John said. "I mean with having to hire a lawyer and an investigator to research who the gold might belong to if it's there."

"It's there."

"Jinx." Katrina punched Murphy's shoulder.

"Then we had to get the property lines surveyed. Then we needed a permit from the Environmental Protection Agency people so we could dig. I sure hope it's all been worth it," Sonia said.

"It's there." Murphy and Katrina blurted in unison. "Jinx." Murphy fake punched her arm.

* * *

There was a slight breeze and it was drizzling an hour later when they were standing at the edge of a freshly-excavated hole at the base of the high ridge directly under Willy's Tree.

Murphy's family and Katrina were joined by Lieutenant Burnett from the Juneau Police. He was a tall man with broad shoulders wearing a long gray trench coat and a floppy brimmed hat that didn't appear waterproof. Sergeant Colwell, a stout, mustached man, stood next to him wearing a clear poncho over his uniform. Mrs. Sutter and a few of the women from the rescue armada joined them.

Murphy knew Randy Green, the tall, slim excavator operator. He was an assistant wrestling coach at the grade school known for his constant encouragement and his permanent lopsided smile.

Randy swung his bucket away from the hole and shut down the excavator, hopped out and approached the spectators. "If the readings are correct, we should use shovels from here on."

John and Randy jumped into the hole and began to remove dirt with hand shovels. In a matter of minutes, everyone heard the unmistakable clang of metal hitting metal. After some hurried scrapping, a rusted lid was revealed.

The men continued to dig until they completely exposed a deteriorating container the size of a large suitcase. It was encircled with bands of riveted steel held in place with a heavy bolt, and that was held secure by a large, decaying padlock.

Randy went to his truck and returned with a short-handled sledgehammer. He handed it to Murphy and smiled. "You should be the one to open it, son."

Murphy took the hammer and glanced at Katrina before jumping into the hole. He positioned himself and swung hard

171

at the lock. Clang, the hammer bounced off the old lock. He swung again. Crunch, the lock broke.

It took both Randy and John to force the bolt to remove the bands. Finally, the container was ready to open. The men made room for Murphy who grabbed the lid with both hands and flung it open.

"Rocks!" A gasp escaped everyone's lips. The case was full of rocks.

After moments of shock and regret, most of the spectators drifted away giving the family space. Randy politely busied himself at his truck. Lieutenant Barnett and Sergeant Colwell handed business cards to John and excused themselves.

John and Sonia stood arm and arm. Katrina stood alone. Hogan curled into a ball at her feet. Murphy stood over the box, hands on his hips. His brow was furrowed; his hair slicked to his skull. He stared at the rusty box of rocks, remembering Blackwell's poem.

Why the poem? It's out of place. Could it be a clue? What am I missing?

He repeated the poem in his mind as it played like a reel.

Be discouraged not
When my burden causes fraught
Like Davey Jones deep under
Stay the quest for thine plunder.

It rolled across his mind. Over and over.

Be discouraged not
When my burden causes fraught
When my burden

My burden. Murphy sprang into action. He bounded out of the hole and rushed to Randy and had a hurried conversation with him before returning to stand with the others.

Randy Green mounted his excavator and started it and a huge cloud of black diesel fumes exploded from the exhaust pipe. He swung the bucket back over the hole.

"What's happening, son?" Sonia asked.

"When overburden causes your fraught." He yelled to be heard over the noise of the digging machine.

Suddenly John grabbed him by the shoulders and shook him. "Overburden." He yelled. "Like in gold mining, overburden is the dirt and rocks that cover the gold."

"The gold's under the rocks!" Katrina yelled.

They hugged one another. The celebration ended quickly when they heard a loud scraping noise.

Randy's bucket scooped the box of rocks out of the hole. Murphy saw more metal was now exposed.

Murphy and his dad jumped down and used their hands to brush the dirt away. They quickly unearthed an exact replica of the first box, complete with a metal band, connecting rod and sturdy lock.

Randy Green passed down the hammer.

Epilogue

A year after Fisher, Carlson and the gang of thieves were incarcerated, Murphy, his parents and Hogan stood with Katrina and her dad, Jerry, in front of a beautiful new building near the shore of Gastineau Channel. The sun was out and the sky was a deep indigo blue. A slight breeze blew over the gathered crowd. A red ribbon stretched across the walkway in front of the wide glass doors. The Mayor of Juneau, William Smallwood IV, stood between Murphy and his family and Katrina and her dad.

Mayor Smallwood stepped forward and waved to the crowd as he strode to the small wooden podium.

"Welcome, ladies and gentlemen, to the grand opening of Douglas' Family Aquatic Center. This wonderful facility has been made possible through the generosity of one family here in Douglas who donated the funds to build this new complex for the good people of our cities." He glanced at Murphy. "You're going to let us Juneau folks use it, too? Right, son?"

Murphy grinned and nodded vigorously.

The mayor pantomimed wiping sweat from his brow. "Well, that's a relief and I know that I, for one, can't wait. Without further ado, I introduce Murphy Delgado." The mayor motioned Murphy over and began to clap as the crowd joined in.

Murphy hesitantly stepped to the microphone with Hogan beside him. He turned and beckoned Katrina. She frowned and shook her head.

Murphy turned to the crowd. He noticed Randy Green in the back row, smiling. Murphy waved. He saw Mrs. Sutter with many of her fellow Judo practitioners. The Connolly sisters were there with Helen Parks and Sandra Evans. He recognized the red-headed woman and a few of the others who were there that night at the lagoon. He saw Mr. Wallace and was thankful he had left his mower at home. Mrs. Ivanov was walking Fluffy in the grass at the back of the crowd. Mr. Troutman, his wrestling coach, was in the front row and flashed Murphy a double thumbs up. He was flanked on both sides by a group of Murphy's school friends, including Mikey who smiled and shrugged. Murphy gave him an I told you so look and crossed his eyes.

"Um, um, well, as you all know, I mean, I guess everyone knows about the gold. We tried to give it back to the relatives of the rightful owners but it was impossible to find them." Murphy paused and swallowed nervously. He had never spoken in front of a crowd.

Hogan reared up, put his huge paws on Murphy's shoulders, and licked him in the face. "Get down, Hoge, yuck." He pushed him off and wiped his face with a sleeve. Everyone erupted into laughter.

When the merriment subsided, Murphy wasn't as nervous. "So anyway, a bad man, unfortunately, he was one of my dad's relatives." He pointed at his parents. "From like a hundred years ago. Well, he wrote that the gold should be used for good. So, we used it for good."

He swept his arm toward the gleaming new building. "I hope everyone likes it. Thanks."

Mayor Smallwood stood beside him and spoke. "Thanks to the bravery and tenacity of this young man, a mystery was solved and our communities benefit greatly. Let's give him a big hand."

The dozens of people clapped and hooted. Murphy was embarrassed and he tried to step back but the mayor had a hand on his back.

After the applause died, Murphy spoke again. "I couldn't have done any of this without my cousin, er, friend ..." He turned around. His eyes searched for Katrina. She was gone and Uncle Jerry was gone as well. His parents shrugged.

Murphy turned back to the audience. "Irene Adler," he shouted and laughed before stepping down from the podium.

Mayor Smallwood and Murphy approached the long red ribbon. The mayor handed him an enormous pair of scissors that Murphy took in both hands. He was distracted by the loud roar of an engine. He glanced toward the parking lot and glimpsed the flash of a bright blue Harley Davidson motorcycle. He caught the sight of Katrina behind her dad as the tires squealed on the pavement. He thought he heard her laughter over the roar of the engine as they raced away.

Murphy cut the ribbon, rushed to the double doors and threw them wide open. Before anyone moved, he ran back to the podium, grabbed the microphone and pointed at the cluster of his friends standing in the front row.

He yelled into the mic, "I told you I saw pirates! Ha, ha, and I proved it. ARRRRGGGGGG! Come on. Let's go walk the plank."

The crowd surged into the new facility. As the last person entered, Hogan squirmed inside, his rump and stubby tail disappearing as the door closed.

Murphy and the Mystery of the Outlaw Gold Mine

Chapter 1

Murphy jerked in horror as the creature landed on his neck. He screamed when it flopped onto his face and omitted a high-pitched squeal next to his ear.

He frantically swatted the darkness in his panic, twisting and shaking to get away, but his body was wedged in place. He dropped his phone and covered his face with one hand, flailing at the darkness with the other. To his relief, he was able to throw the beast off of his head. Despite his heavy breathing he could hear his assailant flopping and scuffling nearby. He shivered at the prospect of another attack.

It's just a bat. Calm down, breathe.

He inhaled deeply, counting to three as he drew air into his lungs, then he slowly exhaled to the count of three and repeated it. It was a technique Coach Troutman taught him in Junior wrestling class. It helped calm his panic when he was caught in a tight hold.

He wasn't afraid of bats, but alone in the dark in a tight space was a whole other thing. *What if it's a vampire bat? They don't live in Alaska. But what if?*

He tentatively ran his hands over the ground searching for his phone, still not completely convinced the bat didn't want to suck his blood.

Where's my phone? Did the light go out? I hope I didn't drop it down the …

At that moment, the bat flapped its wings. Murphy cringed as the leathery appendages brush his cheek. He listened as it gained flight. The sound grew fainter and he realized the bat had flown straight down into the chasm.

He gazed after it and noticed a faint glow of light after pushing closer to the edge and peering over the rim. What he saw gave him hope. The cell phone was sitting upside down on a small ledge about an arm's length away.

Murphy dug the toes of his boots into the hard packed earth and inched closer. The Juniper branches dug into his back as protruding rocks pushed into his ribs. His fingers clutched at the air a few inches from it. With his free hand, he blindly searched for something to hold onto, found a thick branch of the Juniper bush and grasped it tightly.

His body inched forward and he tried for his phone again. His fingers only touched it as he pushed and strained with all his might, only needing another inch.

Suddenly, his brain registered a loud cracking sound, like the sound you hear when a limb is torn from a tree, and his body jolted forward.

"No!"

The Juniper branch tore loose in his hand. His body lurched forward; his shoulders hung over the hole and he was slipping into it.

His hands desperately sought purchase on the smooth rock at the top of the opening. His fingers worked feverishly at every small bump and crack, but they couldn't find a safe grip.

Gravity steadily pulled his body into the black void. He tried desperately to dig his toes into the hard earth.

Abruptly, he fell headfirst into the abyss. For a brief moment, his boots hooked the rim but immediately slipped off. He plummeted into the unknown.

"Nooooooooooooo ..."

★ ★ ★

The day's outing had started when Murphy and Katrina stepped from the Mount Roberts tram glass-enclosed car at its spectacular terminus nearly two thousand feet above the historic streets of Juneau, Alaska, the state's capital city.

It was the first day of operation for the tram that spring. The sun was high in the sky on the rare calm and cloudless day.

It was fast becoming a tradition for the locals to take advantage of the first week of operation before the multitude of cruise ship visitors overwhelmed the tiny city and the tram itself. Many hiked the myriads of trails, some came to photograph the spectacular scenery, others to admire the astounding panorama while they enjoyed a picnic lunch. And some came strictly for the thrill of the ride.

Hogan pulled hard at his leash. Murphy leaned back to slow him down but was forced to jog to keep up.

"Slow down, Hoge, we just got here. We have all day."

Hogan wanted to sniff everywhere at once. His pushed-up black nose worked feverishly; his bulging eyes darted in every direction. His tan fur glowed in the sun and his white feet pranced impatiently.

Murphy pulled on the leash. "Hogan, calm down." He raised his voice.

At the mention of his name, Hogan wagged his stubby tail and circled back to lick Murphy's hand.

"Do you smell the flowers?" Katrina called as she began skipping to keep up.

"Yes, it's awesome up here in the spring and the tram is always savage. Scary but so worth it," Murphy replied.

"It's pure adrenalin for six minutes. But I always forget to take selfies." She adjusted her round-lensed, red-tinted sunglasses.

Murphy managed to slow Hogan down to a walk. "I like it."

"Like what?

"Your hair."

"Oh, okay, um, thanks."

"What do you call it?"

"What?"

"The color."

"Indigo." Katrina's hair was tied high in a single pony tail that seemed to erupt from the top of her head. The sun glinted off of its luxurious deep blue.

Modern Pebbles chic. Murphy smirked.

"Can I ask you something?"

She was silent for an uncomfortable pause. "I guess."

"Where did you find neon green hiking boots to match your neon green pants or was it the other way around?" He snickered and stepped away quickly.

"At least I don't order my clothes from Outdoor Nerds are Us."

"Mean." He couldn't help looking down at his tan cargo shorts, brown hiking boots and navy t-shirt.

She smiled and batted her eye lashes.

He grimaced. *I should have known better.*

Katrina changed the subject. "Sorry your mom has the flu and couldn't come. It was nice of her to send us anyway. I feel guilty; maybe we should have stayed home and helped her out."

Murphy was surprised to realize it made him happy that she had referred to his home as her home. She stayed with them so often people thought they were siblings. The two of them found it easier to say they were cousins. It was basically true as their fathers were lifelong friends and the families were extremely close.

"My dad's coming in this afternoon. He said he will nurse her back to health," Murphy reassured her.

"Your dad sure travels a lot."

"What about your dad, he's out crabbing all season."

"Not the same, but I guess." She stopped skipping.

Murphy glanced at her and noticed a distant look in her eyes. They made their way to an observation deck close to the tram's terminal. From there, Murphy could see his home in Douglas across Gastineau Channel. He could see most of Douglas Island and the snowy tops of the Chilkat Mountains in the distance to the west. They enjoyed the vast and beautiful scenery in silent revery for a few minutes before moving on. Even Hogan seemed taken with the amazing vista and he sat quietly beside Murphy.

They passed a gaggle of first graders coming down the path holding onto a rope led by a harried Mrs. Harper. It might have been her first field trip. Murphy knew she was new to the school. Mr. Able, Murphy's friend Mikey's dad, was at the tail end of the rope. Daisey, Mikey's little sister, was second from the end. Murphy waved at Daisey and smiled at Mr. Able as they passed. Mr. Able rolled his eyes and slumped his shoulders. Mr. Able was a policeman during the day and coached a men's boxing club after hours. From his gestures, he had met his match with a half dozen six-year-olds.

They passed the gift shop, the theater, and bar and grill. The tram had delivered them approximately halfway up the nearly four-thousand-foot-high mountain that looms over Juneau far below. They stopped to read the large sign mapping the hiking trail routes. Mount Roberts has a number of trails from easy to difficult. They chose a moderate three-mile trek that would take them through spruce forests, boulder-strewn alpine pastures, moss-covered rock glaciers and ending at a small glacier-fed lake in a picturesque mountain valley. They would wind their way back by a different route that followed the bubbly brook draining from the lake.

They strolled leisurely following the wide gravel pathway through an alpine meadow. Small streams and waterfalls dotted the landscape. Murphy squinted but smiled. He had forgotten his sun glasses, but he didn't care. *What a day.*

Hogan woofed and stood erect. "What is it, boy?" Murphy scratched his ears.

A blur of red fur exploded across the trail only a few yards away. Hogan bolted, jerking Murphy from his feet and ripping the leash from his grasp. He landed on his shoulder and his face at the side of the path.

Murphy sprang to his feet and brushed himself off. He looked just in time to see Hogan's rear end and stubby tail disappear around a tall rock outcropping in the middle of a nearby meadow.

"Hogan, come," he called. Hogan didn't come. Murphy repeated his command.

"Wow." Katrina seemed in awe and amused by what she had just witnessed.

She reached up and pulled a chunk of moss out of Murphy's tawny hair as he examined a small cut on his knee.

"I thought he always did what he was told."

"He usually does but maybe he can't hear me. Wait here. I'll go get him."

He didn't look back and began jogging toward the stone obelisk where he had seen Hogan's white rear end disappear from sight.

He ran across a grassy meadow strewn with boulders and crumbling spires of decaying rock. At first, he tried not to step on the wild flowers but there were too many and he cringed as he trampled through a patch of mountain crocus. The meadows were covered in a vibrant blanket representing a kaleidoscope of color.

Murphy rounded the outcropping where Hogan had disappeared and was immediately confused. Stretched before him was a small sloping valley covered in nothing but moss-covered rocks and flowers. There was absolutely nothing for a dog of Hogan's size to hide behind.

"Hogan, come, boy, come now." He wandered the valley calling loudly. Eventually he retraced his steps and arrived back at the last place they had seen Hogan.

Murphy examined the craggy monolith. It was three times the size of his dad's big SUV and twice as high as the monkey bars at school. The surface was cracked and porous but he didn't see any caves or fissures big enough for a full-grown Boxer to enter. Murphy ran his hands along its surface as though searching for a hidden door. There were low Mountain Juniper bushes growing along the base of the north side. He lay down on his stomach and peered under the lowest branches. There was an overhang and a space big enough for a fox or a dog. Far back under the shelf, he saw a black hole in the ground.

Could this be the fox's den? Did Hogan follow it?

He peeled off his backpack, set it against the rock and squeezed his head and shoulders under the pungent branches, inching toward the dark opening. It was a tight fit and he struggled as the low branches dug into his back and tugged at his t-shirt. Grabbing the base of the bush, he pulled himself toward the edge of the opening, digging his boots into the dirt and inching forward.

Murphy repeatedly called for Hogan. When he was close enough to see over the edge of the darkened void, he struggled to retrieved his phone from his back pocket and turn on the light.

There was a steep-sided opening descending sharply into the darkness about the size of a bicycle tire.

No way a fox went down there. How would it get out?

Murphy noticed another opening at the other side of the hole. It was a wide crack in the rock that immediately turned a corner he couldn't see around. A small tuft of reddish fur was caught in a rock crack where the opening disappeared. Both openings were small but Hogan could fit in either.

Did he follow the fox?

"Hogan!" He yelled down the hole, then into the opening across from him, and held his breath to listen. Nothing. A rock poked into his thigh and he twisted to relieve his discomfort. His shoulder scraped the ceiling. That's when the bat attacked.

* * *

Murphy slid rather than fell for what seemed like minutes but in reality, was only a few seconds. He managed to twist his body so he was descending feet first. His boots smacked a solid surface, his knees buckled and his butt hit. He grunted loudly and toppled to his side.

Glossary of Nautical Terms

Afloat 1. (of a vessel) Floating freely (not aground or sunk). The term may also be used more generally of any floating object or person. 2. In service, even if not currently underway, but not stranded, crewless, in repair, or under construction (e.g.) "the company has ten ships afloat"

Afore 1. In, on, or toward the fore or front of a vessel. 2. In front of a vessel.

Aft 1. Toward the stern or rear of a vessel. Contrast fore. 2. The portion of the vessel behind the middle area of the vessel.

Aground Resting on or touching the ground or land either intentionally or deliberately, such as in a drying harbor, as opposed to afloat. The bottom of a body of water.

Ahead Forward of the bow.

Alongside By the side of a ship or pier.

Amidships 1. A position halfway along the length of a ship or boat. 2. A position halfway between the port and starboard sides of the ship or boat, as in "helm amidships" when the rudder is in line with the keel.

Anchor Any object designed to prevent or slow the drift of a ship, attached to the ship by a line or chain; usually a metal hook or plow-like object designed to grip the solid seabed under the body of water.

Armada Group of vessels.

Beam The width of a vessel at its widest point or a point alongside the ship at the midpoint of its length.

Board To step onto, climb onto or otherwise enter a vessel.

Boat Any small craft or vessel designed to float on and provide transport over or under water.

Boathook A pole with a blunt tip and a hook on the end, sometimes with a ring on its opposite end to which a line may be attached. Typically used in docking and undocking a boat with its hook used to pull a boat towards a dock as well as to reach into the water to help people catch a buoy or other floating objects or to reach people in the water.

Bow The front of the vessel.

Bulkhead An upright wall within the hull of a ship, particularly a watertight, load-bearing wall.

Bouy A floating object, usually anchored at a given position and fulfilling one of a number of uses, recognized by a defined shape and color for each, including aids to navigation, warnings of danger such as submerged wrecks or divers, or for attaching mooring lines, crab pots, or other items.

Cabin An enclosed room on a deck or flat, especially one used as living quarters.

Capsize (of a vessel) To list so severely that the vessel rolls over, exposing the keel.

Cleat A stationary device used to secure a rope (or line) aboard a vessel.

Companionway A raised and windowed hatchway in a ship's deck with a ladder leading below and hooded entrance hatch to the main cabins.

Craft A ship or other vessel.

Deck 1. The top of a ship or vessel. 2. Any of the structures forming the horizontal levels of a ship or vessel.

Dog (To dog down.) Manually tighten or lock a mechanical device such as a latch.

Dingy A type of a small boat, often carried or towed as a ship's boat by a larger vessel.

Dock An American usage, a fixed structure attached to shore to which a vessel is secured when in port, generally synonymous with pier and wharf.

Ebb Flow of the tide as it retreats.

Fast Fastened or held firmly (e.g., "fast aground" means stuck on the seabed, "made fast" means tied securely.)

Fathom A unit of a length equal to six feet (1.8 m) roughly measured as the distance between a man's outstretched hands.

First Mate The second in command of a commercial vessel.

Flow Inflow of tide from the sea.

Foredeck The deck at the forward end of the ship.

Galleon A large multi-decked sailing ship with a prominent, squared-off end, and raised stern, generally carrying three or more masts.

Gunwale Upper edge of the side of a vessel.

Harbor A place where ships or smaller craft may shelter from the weather, are unloaded/loaded or stored. Harbors can be man-made or natural.

Harbormaster A person in charge of a harbor with powers including the collection of the harbor dues, instructing the masters of vessels where to moor, and overall safety within the area of the harbor, often including pilotage and navigational aids.

Hatch or Hatchway A covered opening in a ship's deck through which cargo can be loaded or access made to a lower deck; the cover to the opening is called the hatch.

Helm A ship's steering mechanism, such as a tiller or ship's wheel.

Hold The lower part of the interior of the ship's hull, especially when considered as storage space, as for cargo.

Hull The shell and framework of the basic flotation-oriented part of the ship.

Keel The principal central longitudinal structural member of a hull, positioned at or close to the lowest point of the hull. Where the keel protrudes below the surface of the hull, it provides hydrodynamic resistance to the lateral forces that give rise to leeway. A ballast keel of (typically) lead or cast iron may be fastened underneath the structural keel in sailing vessels to provide stability and usually providing additional hydrodynamic resistance effects.

Keel Haul A torture consisting of dragging a person under the keel of a ship.

Klaxon Loud horn or alarm.

Knot A unit of speed equivalent to one nautical mile (1.8510 km, 1.1508 mi) per hour.

Lifeboat A small boat kept on board a vessel and used to take crew and passengers to safety in the event of the vessel being abandoned.

Line The correct nautical term for the majority of the cordage or "ropes" used on a vessel.

Main deck The uppermost continuous deck extending from bow to stern.

Mast The vertical poll on a ship that supports sails or rigging.

Moor 1. To attach a ship to a mooring bouy or post. 2. To dock a ship. 3. To secure a vessel with a cable or anchor.

Nautical Of or pertaining to sailors, seamanship, or navigation; maritime.

Oar A pole, usually of wood, with a blade at one end and a handle at the other, which is pivoted on a fulcrum on the side of a boat to provide propulsion by moving the blade through the water.

Offshore 1. Moving away from shore. 2. (of a wind) Blowing from the land to the sea.

Paddle Steamer A steamship or steamboat powered by a steam engine that drives paddle wheels to propel the craft through the water.

Painter A rope attached to the bow of a vessel used to make the vessel fast to the dock or a larger vessel, including when towed.

Pier A raised structure, typically supported by widely spread piles or pillars, used industrially for loading and unloading ships, and recreationally for walking and mooring private craft.

Port The left side of the ship or vessel. Towards the left-handed side of the ship facing forward. Denoted with a red light at night.

Rigging The system of masts and lines on ships and other vessels.

Rudder A steering device that is placed aft and pivoted about a (usually vertical) axis to generate a yawing moment from hydrodynamic forces that act on the rudder blade when it is angled to the flow of water over it.

Sail A piece of fabric attached to a vessel and arranged such that it causes the wind to drive the vessel along. Sails are typically attached to the vessels via a combination of mast, spars, and ropes.

Second Mate An officer of the deck department of a merchant vessel in command of watchkeeping and customarily the ship's navigation.

Seiner A fishing vessel rigged to use seine net to catch fish.

Spar Traditionally a wooden pole used in the rigging of sailing ships to support its sails.

Shipwreck 1. The remains of a ship that has sunk. 2. The remains of a ship that has run aground such that she is no longer seaworthy.

Sidewheel A side-mounted paddle wheel used for propulsion by a paddle steamer.

VHF Radio Very High Frequency. Two-way radio, common on commercial and private vessels worldwide.

Wake A turbulence in the water behind a moving vessel.

Waterline The line where the hull of a ship meets the water's surface.

Wharf A Structure on the shore of a harbor or on the bank of a river or canal where ships may dock to load and unload cargo or passengers.

Williwaw A sudden and violent wind blowing down the mountains toward the coast, found in the far north or south waters, including Alaska.

Yard A spar on a mast from which sails are attached.

Yardarm The very end of the yard. Often mistaken for a yard, which refers to the entire spar.

Yaw A vessel's rotational motion about the vertical axis, causing the fore and aft ends to swing from side to side.

About the Author

Bradford D. Smith grew up as an only child amongst a household of Huskies and Malamutes. At times, he thought they were his siblings. From the age of two, he lived in Atlin, British Columbia, a historic gold mining town nestled deep in the wilderness just south of the Yukon Border and connected to Alaska by the Juneau ice field.

Brad grew up without radio or television in a time before video machines and home computers were common. Books and reading were important entertainment and in the dark, subzero winter months, they became paramount to the sound mental survival of many. Brad's mom read to him before he was born and throughout his childhood. This instilled an intense curiosity deep within him and an insatiable appetite to satisfy it.

Brad read everything he could find and at a young age, he was reading books his mother enjoyed about arctic explorers, prospectors, trappers and first nations people.

His latest book, a young adult mystery, *Murphy and the Mystery of the Black Skull,* was shaped by his own fascination with the mystery genre as a young adult. Updated to fit today's times, he leans heavily on the style of writing he himself enjoyed as a young teen. This book is sprinkled with real world places and the author's love of history is quickly exposed in this fast-paced adventure.

Brad has lived and worked in many places across Alaska over the years including Juneau. He still works in Arctic Alaska seasonally and lives with his wife in central BC, Canada with their pack of dogs.

Brad is currently working on the second book in the Williwaw Mystery Series, *Murphy and the Mystery of the Outlaw Gold Mine.*

www.bradfordsmithauthor.com

www.ingramcontent.com/pod-product-compliance
Lightning Source LLC
Chambersburg PA
CBHW061306210726
48293CB00003B/1141